## "Where's your daughter right now?" Beck asked.

His tone alone would have alarmed her, but there was more than a sense of urgency in his expression.

"Aubrey's with her nanny. Why?"

"Because I was just trying to put myself in the killer's place. If he came here to scare you off and it didn't work, then what will he do next?" His stare was a warning.

Faith's heart dropped to her knees.

Beck took a step toward her. "He might try to use your daughter to get to you."

"Oh, God." Faith grabbed her phone and prayed that it wasn't too late to keep her baby safe.

25 years of INTRIGUE

Dear Harlequin Intrigue Reader,

In honor of two very special events, the Harlequin Intrigue editorial team has planned exceptional promotions to celebrate throughout 2009. To kick off the year, we're celebrating Harlequin Books' 60th Diamond Anniversary with DIAMONDS AND DADDIES, an exciting four-book miniseries featuring protective dads and their extraordinary proposals to four very lucky women. Rita Herron launches the series with *Platinum Cowboy* next month.

Later in the year Harlequin Intrigue celebrates its own 25th anniversary. To mark the event we've asked reader favorites to return with their most popular series.

• Debra Webb has created a new COLBY AGENCY trilogy. This time out, Victoria Colby-Camp will need to enlist the help of her entire staff of agents for her own family crisis.

• You can return to 43 LIGHT STREET with Rebecca York and join Caroline Burnes on another crime-solving mission with Familiar the Black Cat Detective.

• Next stop: WHITEHORSE, MONTANA with B.J. Daniels for more Big Sky mysteries with a new family. Meet the Corbetts—Shane, Jud, Dalton, Lantry and Russell.

Because we know our readers love following trace evidence, we've created the new continuity KENNER COUNTY CRIME UNIT. Whether collecting evidence or tracking down leads, lawmen and investigators have more than their jobs on the line, because the real mystery is one of the heart. Pick up *Secrets in Four Corners* by Debra Webb this month, and don't miss any one of the terrific stories to follow in this series.

And that's just a small selection of what we have planned to thank our readers.

We'd love to hear from you, and hope you enjoy all of our special promotions this year.

Happy reading, and happy anniversary, Harlequin Books!

Sincerely,

Denise Zaza
Senior Editor
Harlequin Intrigue

# DELORES FOSSEN

# BRANDED BY THE SHERIFF

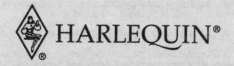

TORONTO • NEW YORK • LONDON
AMSTERDAM • PARIS • SYDNEY • HAMBURG
STOCKHOLM • ATHENS • TOKYO • MILAN • MADRID
PRAGUE • WARSAW • BUDAPEST • AUCKLAND

To Debbie Gafford, thanks for always being there for me.

Recycling programs
for this product may
not exist in your area.

ISBN-13: 978-0-373-69377-1
ISBN-10:    0-373-69377-X

BRANDED BY THE SHERIFF

# ABOUT THE AUTHOR

Imagine a family tree that includes Texas cowboys, Choctaw and Cherokee Indians, a Louisiana pirate and a Scottish rebel who battled side by side with William Wallace. With ancestors like that, it's easy to understand why Texas author and former air force captain Delores Fossen feels as if she were genetically predisposed to writing romances. Along the way to fulfilling her DNA destiny, Delores married an air force top gun who just happens to be of Viking descent. With all those romantic bases covered, she doesn't have to look too far for inspiration.

## Books by Delores Fossen

HARLEQUIN INTRIGUE

*Five-Alarm Babies
**Texas Paternity
†Texas Paternity: Boots and Booties

# CAST OF CHARACTERS

**Beckett "Beck" Tanner**—Sheriff of LaMesa Springs, Texas. There's bad blood between him and the new assistant district attorney, Faith Matthews. But their old family feud doesn't cool the white-hot attraction he has for Faith or the instant fatherly connection he feels with her baby, Aubrey.

**Faith Matthews**—Ten years ago, she was run out of town. Now, her old secrets and her family's shady reputation could threaten the new life she hopes to build. When her child's safety is put in question, she has no choice but to rely on Beck, the man she's always been attracted to—an attraction that fuels new dangers.

**Aubrey Matthews**—Faith's sixteen-month-old daughter. She's too young to understand the dangerous secrets her mother is hiding.

**Corey Winston**—Beck's deputy doesn't seem pleased about Faith's homecoming.

**Sherry Matthews**—Faith's sister was murdered. Is her killer now after Faith? And why?

**Nolan Wheeler**—Sherry's conman ex shows up in LaMesa Springs just as someone attempts to kill Faith.

**Darin Matthews**—Faith's troubled brother was suspected of murdering his sister and mother, but Faith believes he's innocent and wants to clear her brother's name.

**Pete Tanner**—Beck's philandering brother has secrets of his own.

**Nicole Tanner**—Pete's wife. She's jealous because she believes Faith had an affair with her husband. Just how far would Nicole go to make sure Faith doesn't stay in town?

**Roy Tanner**—Beck's father. He's protective of his family and doesn't want Faith around to remind everyone of the painful past.

# Chapter One

*LaMesa Springs, Texas*

A killer was in the house.

Sheriff Beck Tanner drew his weapon and eased out of his SUV. He hadn't planned on a showdown tonight, but he was ready for it.

Beck stopped at the edge of the yard that was more dirt than grass. He listened for a moment.

The light in the back of the small Craftsman-style house indicated someone was there, but he didn't want that someone sneaking out and ambushing him. After all, Darin Matthews had already claimed two victims, his own mother and sister. Since this was Darin's family home, Beck figured sooner or later the man would come back.

Apparently he had.

Around him, the January wind whipped through the bare tree branches. That was the only sound Beck could hear. The house was at the end of the sparsely populated County Line Road, barely in the city limits and a full half mile away from any neighboring house.

There was a hint of smoke in the air, and thanks to

a hunter's moon, Beck spotted the source: the rough stone chimney anchored against the left side of the house. Wispy gray coils of smoke rose into the air, the wind scattering them almost as quickly as they appeared.

He inched closer to the house and kept his gun ready.

His boots crunched on the icy gravel of the driveway. No garage. No car. Just a light stabbing through the darkness. Since the place was supposed to be vacant, he'd noticed the light during a routine patrol of the neighborhood. Beck had also glanced inside the filmy bedroom window and spotted discarded clothes on the bed.

The bedroom wasn't the source of the light though. It was coming from the adjacent bathroom and gave him just enough illumination to see.

Staying in the shadows, Beck hurried through the yard and went to the back of the house. He tried to keep his footsteps light on the wooden porch, but each rickety board creaked under his weight. He knew the knob would open because the lock was broken. He'd discovered that two months earlier when he checked out the place after the murder of the home's owner.

Beck eased open the door just a fraction and heard the water running in the bathroom. "A killer in the shower," he said to himself. All in all, not a bad place for an arrest.

He made his way through the kitchen and into the living room. All the furniture was draped in white sheets, giving the place an eerie feel.

Beck had that same eerie feeling in the pit of his stomach.

He'd been sheriff of LaMesa Springs for eight years,

since he'd turned twenty-four, and he'd been the deputy for the two years before that. But because his town wasn't a hotbed for serious crime, this would be the first time he'd have to take down a killer.

The thought had no sooner formed in his head when the water in the bathroom stopped. He had to make his move now.

Beck gripped his pistol, keeping it aimed.

He nudged the ajar bathroom door with the toe of his boot, and sticky, warm steam and dull, milky light spilled over him.

Since the bathroom was small, he could take in the room in one glance. Outdated avocado tile—some cracked and chipped. A claw-footed tub encased by an opaque shower curtain. There was one frosted glass window to his right that was too small to use to escape.

Beck latched on to the curtain and gave it a hard jerk to the left. The metal hooks rattled, and the sheet of yellowed vinyl slithered around the circular bar that supported it.

"Sheriff Beck Tanner," he identified himself.

But his name died on his lips when he saw the person standing in the tub. It certainly wasn't Darin Matthews.

It was a wet, naked woman.

A scream bubbled up from her throat. Beck cursed. He didn't know which one of them was more surprised.

Well, she wasn't armed. That was the first thing he noticed after the "naked" part. There wasn't a gun anywhere in sight. Just her.

Suddenly, that seemed more than enough.

Water slid off her face, her entire body, and her midnight-black hair clung to her neck and shoulders.

Because he considered himself a gentleman, Beck tried not to notice her small, firm breasts and the triangular patch of hair at the juncture of her thighs.

But because he was a man, and because she was there right in front of him, he noticed despite his efforts to stop himself.

"Beckett Tanner," she spat out like profanity. She swept her left hand over various parts to cover herself while she groped for the white towel dangling over the nearby sink. "What the devil are you doing here?"

Did he know her? Because she obviously knew him.

Beck examined her face and picked through all that wet hair and water to see her features.

Oh, hell.

She was obviously older than the last time he'd seen her, which was...when? Just a little more than ten years ago when she was eighteen. Since then, her body and face had filled out, but those copper brown eyes were the same.

The last time he'd seen those eyes, she'd been silently hurtling insults at him. She was still doing that now.

"Faith Matthews." Beck grumbled. "What the devil are *you* doing here?"

She draped the towel in front of her and stepped from the tub. "I own the place."

Yeah. She did. Thanks to her mother's and sister's murders. Since her mother had legally disowned Faith's brother, the house had passed to Faith by default.

"The DA said you wanted to keep moving back quiet," Beck commented. "But he also said you wouldn't arrive in town until early next month."

Beck figured he'd need every minute of that month,

too, so he could prepare his family for Faith's return. It was going to hit his sister-in-law particularly hard. That, in turn, meant it'd hit him hard.

What someone did to his family, they did to him.

And Faith Matthews had done a real number on the Tanners.

"I obviously came early." As if in a fierce battle with the terry cloth, she wound the towel around her.

"I didn't see your car," he pointed out.

She huffed. "Because I took a taxi from the Austin airport, all right? My car arrives tomorrow. Now that I've explained why I'm in my own home and how I got here, please tell me why you're trespassing."

She sounded like a lawyer. And was. Or rather a lawyer who was about to become the county's new assistant district attorney.

Beck had tried to convince the DA to turn down her job application, but the DA said she was the best qualified applicant and had hired her. That was the reason she was moving back. She wasn't moving back alone, either. She had a kid. A toddler named Aubrey, he'd heard. Not that motherhood would change his opinion of her. That opinion would always be low. And because LaMesa Springs was the county seat, that meant Faith would be living right under his nose, again. Worse, he'd have to work with her to get cases prosecuted.

Yeah, he needed that month to come to terms with that.

"I'm *trespassing* because I thought your brother was here," he explained. "The clerk at the convenience store on Sadler Street said he saw someone matching Darin's description night before last. The Rangers are still analyzing the surveillance video, and when they're done, I figure it'll be a match. So I came here because I wanted to arrest a killer."

"An *alleged* killer," she corrected. "Darin is innocent." The towel slipped, and he caught a glimpse of her right breast again. Her rose-colored nipple, too. She quickly righted the towel and mumbled something under her breath. "Before I got in the shower, I checked the doors and windows and made sure they were all locked. How'd you get in?"

"The back lock's broken. I noticed it when I came out here with the Texas Rangers. They assisted me with the investigation after your mother was killed."

Her intense stare conveyed her displeasure with his presence. "And you just happened to be in the neighborhood again tonight?"

Beck made sure his scowl conveyed some displeasure, too. "As I already said, I want to arrest a killer. I figure Darin will eventually come here. You did. So I've been driving by each night on my way home from work to see if he'll turn up."

She huffed and walked past him. Not a good idea. The doorway was small, and they brushed against each other, her butt against his thigh.

He ignored the pull he felt deep within his belly.

Yes, Faith was attractive, always had been, but she'd come within a hair of destroying his family. No amount of attraction would override that.

Besides, Faith had been his brother's one-night stand. She'd slept with a married man, and that encounter had nearly ruined his brother's marriage.

That alone made her his enemy.

Faith snatched up her clothes from the bed. "Well,

now that you know Darin's not here, you can leave the same way you came in."

"I will. First though, I need to ask some questions." In the back of his mind, he wondered if that was a good idea. She was only a few feet away…and naked under the towel. But Beck decided it was best to put his discomfort aside and worry less about her body and more about getting a killer off the streets.

"When's the last time you saw your brother?" he asked, without waiting to see if she'd agree to the impromptu interrogation.

With a death grip on the towel, she stared at him. Frowned. The frown deepened with each passing second. "Go stand over there," she said, pointing to the pair of front windows that were divided by a bare scarred oak dresser. "And turn your back. I want to get dressed, and I'd rather not do that with you gawking at me."

It was true. He had indeed gawked, and he wasn't proud of it. But then he wasn't proud of the way she'd stirred him up.

"Strange, I hadn't figured you for being modest," he mumbled, strolling toward the windows. He could see his SUV parked out front. It was something to keep his focus on, especially since he didn't want to angle his eyes in any direction in case he caught a glimpse of her naked reflection in the glass.

"Strange?" she repeated as if this insult had actually gotten to her. "I'd say it's equally *strange* that Beckett Tanner would still be making assumptions."

"What does that mean?" he fired back.

Her response was a figure-it-out-yourself grunt. "To answer your original question, I haven't seen Darin in nearly a year." Her words were clipped and angry. "That's in the statement I gave the Texas Rangers two months ago. I'm sure you read it."

Heck, he'd memorized it.

The part about her brother. Her sister's ex. Her estranged relationship with all members of her family. When the Rangers had asked her if Aubrey's father, Faith's own ex, could have some part in this, she'd adamantly denied it, claiming the man had never even seen Aubrey.

All of that had been in her statement, but over the years he'd learned that a written response wasn't nearly as good as the real thing.

"You haven't seen your brother in a long time, yet you don't think he's guilty?"

Silence.

Beck wished he'd waited to ask that particular question because he would have liked to have seen her reaction, but there wasn't any way he was going to turn around while she was dressing.

"Darin wouldn't hurt me," she finally said.

He rolled his eyes. "I'll bet your mother and sister thought the same thing."

"I don't think he killed them." Her opinion wasn't news to him. She had said the same in her interview with the Texas Rangers. "My sister's ex-boyfriend killed them."

Nolan Wheeler. Beck knew him because the man used to live in LaMesa Springs. He was as low-life as they came, and Beck along with the Texas Rangers had been looking for Nolan, who'd seemingly disappeared after giving his statement to the police in Austin.

Well, at least Faith hadn't changed her story over the

past two months. But then Beck hadn't changed his theory. "Nolan Wheeler has alibis for the murders."

"Thin alibis," Faith supplied. "Friends of questionable integrity who'll vouch for him."

"That's more than your brother has. According to what I read about Darin, he's mentally unstable, has been in and out of psychiatric hospitals for years, and he resented your mom and sister. On occasion, he threatened to kill them. He carried through on those threats, though I'll admit he might have had Nolan Wheeler's help."

"Now you think my brother had an accomplice?" Faith asked.

He was betting she had a snarky expression to go along with that snarky question. "It's possible. Darin isn't that organized."

Or that bright. The man was too scatterbrained and perhaps too mentally ill to have conceived a plan to murder two women without witnesses or physical evidence to link him to the crimes. And there was plenty of potential for physical evidence since both victims had been first shot with tranquilizer darts and then strangled. Darin didn't impress him as the sort of man who could carry out multistep murders or remember to wear latex gloves when strangling his victims.

Beck heard an odd sound and risked looking in her direction. She was dressed, thank goodness, in black pants and a taupe sweater. Simple but classy.

The sound had come from her kneeling to open a suitcase. She pulled out a pair of flat black shoes and slipped them on. Faith also took out a plush armadillo before standing, and she clutched onto it when she faced him head-on. She was about five-six. A good eight inches shorter than he was, and with the flats, Beck felt as if he towered over her.

"My brother has problems," she said as if being extra mindful of her word choice. "I don't need to tell you that we didn't have a stellar upbringing, and it affected Darin in a negative way."

It was the old bad blood between them that made him want to remind her that her family was responsible for the poor choices they'd made over the years.

Including what happened that December night ten years ago.

Even now, all these years later, Beck could still see Faith coming out of the Sound End motel with his drunk brother and shoving him into her car. She, however, had been as sober as a judge. Beck should know since, as a deputy at that time, he'd been the one to give her a Breathalyzer. She'd denied having sex with his brother, but there'd been a lot of evidence to the contrary, including his own brother's statement.

"You got something to say to me?" Faith challenged.

Not now. It could wait.

Instead, he glanced at the stuffed baby armadillo. It had a tag from a gift shop in the Austin airport and sported a pink bow around its neck. "I heard you had a baby." Because he was feeling ornery, he glanced at her bare ring finger.

"Yes." Those copper eyes drilled into him. "She's sixteen months old. And, no, I'm not married." The corner of her mouth lifted. Not a smile of humor though. "I guess that just confirms your opinion that I have questionable morals."

He lifted a shoulder and let it stand as his response about that. "You think it's wise to bring a child to LaMesa Springs with a killer at large?"

She mimicked him by lifting her own shoulder, and she let the seconds drag on several moments before she continued. "I have a security company rep coming out first thing in the morning to install some equipment. Once he's finished, I'll call the nanny and have her bring my daughter. We'll stay at the hotel until I have some other repairs and updates done to the house." She glanced around the austere room before her gaze came back to his. "I intend to make this place a home for her."

That's what Beck was afraid she was going to say. This wasn't just about her new job. It was Faith Matthews's homecoming. Something he'd dreaded for ten years. "Even with all the bad memories, you still want to be here?"

Her mouth quivered. "Ah. Is this the part where you tell me I should think of living elsewhere? That I'm not welcome here in *your* town?"

He took a moment with his word selection as well. "You being here will make it hard for my family."

She had the decency to look uncomfortable about that. "I wish I could change that." And she sounded sincere. "But I can't go back and undo history. I can only move forward, and being assistant DA is a dream job for me. I won't walk away from that just because the Tanners don't want me here."

He could tell from the resolve in her eyes that he wasn't going to change her mind. Not that he thought he could anyway. At least he'd gotten his point across that there was still a lot of water under the bridge that his brother and she had built ten years ago in that motel.

But there was another point he had to make. "Even with security measures, it might not be safe for you or your daughter. The man who killed your mother and sister is still out there."

Oh, she was about to disagree. He could almost hear the argument they were about to have. Maybe that wasn't a bad thing. A little air clearing. Except the old stench was so thick between them that it'd take more than an argument to clear it.

She opened her mouth. At the exact moment that Beck caught movement out of the corner of his eye.

Outside the window.

Front yard.

Going on gut instinct, Beck dove at Faith and tackled her onto the bed. He lifted his head and saw the shadowy figure. And worse, it looked as if their *visitor* had a gun pointed right at Faith and him.

# *Chapter Two*

Faith managed a muffled gasp, but she couldn't ask Beck what the heck was going on. The tackle onto the bed knocked the breath from her.

She fought for air and failed. Beck had her pinned down. He was literally lying on her back, and his solid weight pushed her chest right into the hard mattress.

"Someone's out there," Beck warned. "I think he had a gun."

Just like that, she stopped struggling and considered who might be out there. None of the scenarios that came to mind were good. It was too late and too cold for a neighbor to drop by. Besides, she didn't have any nearby neighbors, especially anyone who'd want to pay her a friendly visit. Plus, there was Beck's reaction. He obviously thought this might turn dangerous.

She didn't have to wait long for that to be confirmed.

A sound blasted through the room. Shattering glass. A split-second later, something thudded onto the floor.

"A rock," Beck let her know.

A rock. Not exactly lethal in itself, but the person who'd thrown it could be a threat. And he might have a weapon.

Who had done this?

Better yet, why was Beckett Tanner sheltering her? He had put himself in between her and potential danger, and once she could breathe, Faith figured that maneuver would make more sense than it did now.

Because there was no chance he'd put himself in real harm's way to protect her.

"Get under the bed," Beck ordered. "And stay there."

He rolled off her, still keeping his body between her and the window. Starved for air, Faith dragged in an urgent breath and scrambled to the back side of the mattress so she could drop to the floor. She crawled beneath the bed amid dust bunnies and a few dead roaches.

Staying here tonight, alone, had obviously not been a good idea.

Worse, Faith didn't know why she'd decided at the last minute to stay. Her plan had been to check in to the hotel, to wait for the renovations to be complete and for the new furniture to arrive. But after stepping inside, she thought it was best to exorcise a few demons before trying to make the place "normal." So she'd sent the cab driver on his way, made a fire to warm up the place and got ready for bed.

Now someone had hurled a rock through her window.

There was another crashing sound. Another spray of glass. Another thud. Her stomach tightened into an acidy knot.

Beck got off the bed as well. Dropping onto the floor and staying low, he scurried to what was left of the window and peeked out.

"Can you see who's out there?" she asked.

He didn't answer her, but he did take a sliver-thin cell phone from his jeans pocket and called for backup. For some reason that made Faith's heart pound even harder. If this was a situation that Beck Tanner believed he couldn't handle alone, then it was *bad*.

She thought of Aubrey and was glad her little girl wasn't here to witness this act of vandalism, or whatever it was. Faith also thought of their future, how this would affect it. *If* it would affect it, she corrected. And then she thought of her brother. Was he the one out there in the darkness tossing those rocks? It was a possibility—a remote one—but Beck wouldn't believe it to be so remote.

Her brother, Darin, was Beck's number one murder suspect. She'd read every report she could get her hands on and every newspaper article written about the murders.

She didn't suspect Darin, though. She figured her sister's ex, Nolan Wheeler, was behind those killings. Nolan had a multipage arrest record, and her sister had even taken out a temporary restraining order against him.

For all the good it'd done.

Even with that restraining order, her sister, Sherry, had been murdered near her apartment on the outskirts of Austin. Their mother's death had happened twenty-four hours later in the back parking lot of the seedy liquor store where she worked in a nearby town. The murder had occurred after business hours, within minutes of her mother locking up the shop and going to her car. And even though Faith wasn't close to either of them and hadn't been for years, she'd mourned their loss and the brutal way their lives had ended.

Still staying low, Beck leaned over and studied one

of the rocks. It was smooth, about the size and color of a baked potato, and Faith could see that it had something written on it.

"What does it say?" she asked when Beck didn't read it aloud.

His hesitation seemed to last for hours. "It says, 'Leave or I'll have to kill you, too.'"

Mercy. So it was a threat. Someone didn't want her moving back to town. She watched Beck pick up the second rock.

Beck cursed under his breath. "It's from your brother."

Faith shook her head. "How do you know?"

"Because it says, 'I love you, but I can't stop myself from killing you. Get out,'" Beck grumbled. "I don't know how many people you know who both love you and want you dead. Darin certainly fits the bill. Of course, maybe he just wrote the message and had Wheeler toss it in here for him."

She swallowed hard, and the lump in her throat caused her to ache. God. This couldn't be happening.

Faith forced herself to think this through. Instead of Nolan being Darin's accomplice, Nolan himself could be doing this to set up her brother. Still, that didn't make it less of a threat.

"Listen for anyone coming in through the back door," Beck instructed.

There went her breath again. If Beck had been able to break in, then a determined killer or vandal would have no trouble doing the same.

Because she had to do something other than cower and wait for the worst, Faith crawled to the end of the bed where she'd placed her suitcase. After a few run-ins with Nolan Wheeler, she'd bought a handgun. But she didn't have it with her. However, she did have pepper spray.

She retrieved the slender can from her suitcase and inched out a little so she could see what was going on. Beck was still crouched at the window, and he had his weapon ready and aimed into the darkness.

With that part of the house covered, she shifted her attention to the bedroom door. From her angle, she could see the kitchen, and if the rock thrower took advantage of that broken lock, he'd have to come through the kitchen to get to them. Thankfully, the moonlight piercing through the back windows allowed her to see that the room was empty.

"You don't listen very well," Beck snarled. "I told you to stay put."

She ignored his bark. Faith wouldn't make herself an open target, but she wanted to be in a position to defend herself.

"Do you see anyone out there?" she barked back.

She clamped her teeth over her bottom lip to stop the trembling. Not from fear. She was more angry than afraid. But with the gaping holes in the window, the winter wind was pushing its way through the room, and she was cold.

"No. But if I were a betting man, I'd say your brother's come back to eliminate his one and only remaining sibling—you."

"Maybe the person outside is after you?"

He glanced back at her. So brief. A split-second look. Yet, he conveyed a lot of hard skepticism with that glimpse.

"You're the sheriff," she reminded him. "You must

have made enemies. Besides, my mother and sister have been dead for over two months. If that's Darin or their real killer out there, why would he wait this long to come after me? It's common knowledge that I was living in Oklahoma City and practicing law there for the past few years. Why not just come after me there?"

"A killer doesn't always make sense."

True. But there were usually patterns. Her mother and sister's killer had attacked them when they were alone. He hadn't been bold or stupid enough to try to shoot them with a police officer nearby. Of course, maybe the killer didn't realize that the car out front belonged to Beck, since it was his personal vehicle and not a cruiser. Therefore he wouldn't have known that Beck was there. She certainly hadn't been aware of it when she had been in that shower. Talk about the ultimate shock when she'd seen him standing there.

Her, stark naked.

Him, combing those smoky blue eyes all over her body.

"Dreamy eyes," the girls in school had called him. Dreamy eyes to go with a dreamy body, that toast-brown hair and quarterback's build.

Faith hadn't been immune to Beck's sizzling hot looks, either. She'd looked. But the looking stopped after the night he'd given her a Breathalyzer test at the motel.

A lot of things had stopped that night.

And there was no going back to that place. Even if those dreamy looks still made her feel all warm and willing.

"I hope you're having second and third thoughts about bringing your daughter here," Beck commented. He still had his attention fastened to the front of the house.

She was. But what was the alternative? If this was

Darin or her sister's slimy ex, then where could she take Aubrey so she'd be safe?

Nowhere.

That was a sobering and frightening thought.

But Beck was right about one thing. She needed to rethink this. Not the job. She wasn't going to run away from the job. However, she could do something about making this a safe place for Aubrey. And the first thing she'd do was to catch the person who'd thrown those rocks through her window.

She could start by having the handwriting analyzed. Footprints, too. Heck, she wanted to question the taxi driver to see if he'd told anyone that he'd dropped her off at the house. Someone had certainly learned quickly enough that she was there.

"I think the guy's gotten away by now," Faith let Beck know.

He didn't answer because his phone rang. Beck glanced at the screen and answered with a terse, "Where are you right now?" He paused, no doubt waiting for the answer. "Someone in front of the house threw rocks through the window. Check the area and let me know what you find."

Good. It was backup. If Nolan Wheeler or whoever was still out there, then maybe he'd be caught. Maybe this would all be over within the next few minutes. Then she could deal with this adrenaline roaring through her veins and get on with her life.

Faith waited there with her fingers clutched so tightly around the pepper spray that her hand began to cramp. The minutes crawled by, and they were punctuated by silence and the occasional surly glance from Beck.

He still hated her.

She could see it in his face. He still blamed her for that night with his brother. Part of her wanted to shout the truth of what'd happened, but he wouldn't believe her. Her own mother hadn't. And over the years she'd convinced herself that it didn't matter. That incident had given her a chip on her shoulder, and she'd used that chip and her anger to succeed. Coming back here, getting the job as the assistant district attorney, that was her proof that she'd risen above the albatross of her family's DNA.

"It's me," someone called out, causing her heart to race again.

But Beck obviously wasn't alarmed. He got to his feet and watched the man approach the window.

"I see some tracks," the man announced. "But if anybody's still out here, then he's freezing his butt off and probably hiding in the bushes across the road."

The man poked his face against the hole in the window, and she got a good look at him. It was Corey Winston. He'd been a year behind her in high school and somewhat of a smart mouth. These days, he was Beck's deputy. She'd learned that during her job interview with the district attorney.

Corey's insolent gaze met hers. "Faith Matthews." He used a similar tone to the one Beck had used when he first saw her. "What are you doing back in LaMesa Springs?"

"She's going to be the new assistant district attorney," Beck provided.

That earned her a raised eyebrow from Corey. "Now I've heard everything. You, the ADA? Well, you're not off to a good start. You breeze into town, your first night back, and you're already stirring up trouble, huh?"

The *huh* was probably added to make it sound a little less insulting. But it only riled her more. She'd let jerks like Corey, and Beck, run her out of town ten years earlier, but they wouldn't succeed this time.

She would continue full speed ahead, and if that included arresting her own brother, she'd do it and carry out her lawful duties. Of course, because of a personal conflict, the DA himself would have to prosecute the case, but she would fully cooperate. It helped that she had been estranged from her mother and sister. That wouldn't help with Darin. It would hurt. But duty had to come first here.

Beck reholstered his gun and glanced around at the glass on the floor. "Secure the scene," he told Corey. "Cast at least one of the footprints, and I'll send it to the lab in Austin. We might get lucky."

"You think it's worth it?" Corey challenged. But his defiance went down a notch when Beck stared at him. "It just seems like a lot of trouble to go through considering this was probably done by those Kendrick kids. You know those boys have too much time on their hands and nobody at home to see what they're up to."

"There's a killer on the loose," Beck reminded him.

That reminder, however, didn't stop Corey from scowling at Faith before he turned from the window and got to work. He grumbled something indistinguishable under his breath.

Beck looked at her then. He wasn't exactly sporting a scowl like Corey, but it was close. "I need you to come with me to my office so I can take a statement."

It was standard operating procedure. Something that needed to be done, just in case it had been the killer outside that window. Besides, she didn't want to be alone in the house. Not tonight. Maybe not ever. She would truly have to rethink making this place a home for Aubrey.

Faith grabbed her purse and got ready to go.

"I don't believe it was the Kendrick kids who threw those rocks," Beck said to her.

That stopped her in her tracks. "You think it was Darin?" she challenged.

"If not Darin, then let's play around with your assumption, that your mom and sister's killer was Sherry's ex, Nolan Wheeler." He hitched his thumb toward the broken glass. "If Nolan was outside that window tonight, he could want to do you harm."

She shook her head. "Stating the obvious here, but if that's true, why wait until now?"

"Because you were here, alone. Or so he thought. You were an easy target."

Faith zoomed in on the obvious flaw in his theory. "And his motive for wanting me dead?"

"Maybe Nolan thinks you'll use your new job to come after him for the two murders. He might even think that's why you've come back."

She opened her mouth to deny it, but she couldn't. In fact, that's exactly the way Nolan would think.

Other than in confidence to her boss, Faith hadn't announced to anyone in Oklahoma that she had accepted the job in LaMesa Springs.

Not until this morning.

This morning, she'd also called LaMesa Springs'

DA to tell him she would be arriving. She had arranged for renovations and a security system for the house. She'd made lots and lots of calls, and anyone could have found out her plans.

Anyone, including Nolan.

"Where's your daughter right now?" Beck asked. His tone alone would have alarmed her, but there was more than a sense of urgency in his expression.

"Aubrey's still in Oklahoma with her nanny. Why?"

"Because I was just trying to put myself in Nolan's place. If he came here to scare you off and it didn't work, then what will he do next?" His stare was a warning. "If he's got an accomplice or if it was his accomplice who just tossed those rocks, that means one of them could be here in LaMesa Springs and the other could be in Oklahoma."

Her heart dropped to her knees.

Beck took a step toward her. "Either Darin or Nolan might try to use your daughter to get to you."

"Oh, God."

Faith grabbed her phone from her purse and prayed that it wasn't too late to keep Aubrey safe.

# *Chapter Three*

By Beck's calculation, Faith had been pacing in his office for three hours while she waited for her daughter to arrive. Even when she'd been on the phone, which was a lot, or while giving her official statement to him, she still paced. And while she did that, she continued to check her delicate silver watch.

The minutes were probably dragging by for her.

They certainly were for him.

Beck tried to keep himself occupied with routine paperwork and notes on his current cases. Normally he liked keeping busy. But this wasn't a normal night.

Faith Matthews was in his office, mere yards away, and sooner or later he was going to have to break the news to his family that she'd returned. Since it was going on midnight, Beck had opted for later, but he knew, with the gossip mill always in full swing, that if he didn't tell his father, brother and sister-in-law by morning—early morning, at that—then they'd find out from some other source.

As if she knew what he was thinking, Faith tossed him a glance from over her shoulder.

Despite the vigor of her pacing, she was exhausted. Her eyes were sleep-starved, and her face was pale and tight with tension. On some level he understood that tension.

Her daughter might be in danger, and she was waiting for the little girl to arrive with her nanny and the Texas Ranger escort from the Austin airport. Beck hadn't had the opportunity to be around many babies, but he figured the parental bond was strong, and the uncertainty was driving Faith crazy.

"You're staring at me," she grumbled.

Yeah. He was.

Beck glanced back at his desk, but the glance didn't take. For some stupid reason, his attention went straight back to Faith. To her tired expression. Her tight muscles. The still damp hair that she hadn't had a chance to dry after her shower.

Noticing her hair immediately made him uncomfortable. But then so did Faith. Dealing with a scrawny eighteen-year-old was one thing, but Faith was miles away from being that girl. She was poised and polished, even now despite the damp hair. A woman in every sense of the word.

Hell. That made him uncomfortable, too.

"I figure you're having second thoughts about accepting the ADA job," he grumbled, hoping conversation would help. It was a fishing expedition since she'd kept her thoughts to herself the entire time she had been waiting for her daughter and the nanny to arrive.

"You wish," she tossed at him. "The DA and the city council want me here, and I have to just keep telling myself that not everyone in town hates me like the Tanners."

Okay. No second thoughts. Well, not any that she

would likely voice to him. She had dug in her heels, unlike ten years ago when she'd left town running. Part of him, the part he didn't want to acknowledge, admired her for not wavering in her plans. She certainly hadn't shown much backbone or integrity ten years ago.

She flipped open her cell phone again and pressed redial. Beck didn't have to ask who she was calling. He knew it was the nanny. Faith had called the woman at least every half hour.

"How much longer?" Faith asked the moment the woman apparently answered. The response made her relax a bit, and she seemed to breathe easier when she added, "See you then."

"Good news?" he asked when she didn't share.

"They'll be here in about fifteen minutes." She raked her hair away from her face. "I should have just gone to the airport to meet them."

"The Texas Rangers didn't want you to do that," Beck reminded her, though he was certain she already knew that. The Ranger lieutenant and her new boss, the DA, had ordered her to stay put at the sheriff's office.

The order was warranted. It was simply too big of a risk for her to go gallivanting all over central Texas when there might be a killer on her trail.

"So what's the plan when your daughter arrives?" Beck asked.

"Since the Texas Rangers said they'll be providing security, we'll check in to the hotel on Main Street." She didn't hesitate, which meant, in addition to the calls and pacing, she'd obviously given it plenty of thought. "Then tomorrow morning, I can start putting some security measures in place."

He'd overheard her conversations with the Rangers about playing bodyguard and the other conversation about those measures. She was having a high-tech security system installed in her childhood home. In a whispered voice, she'd asked the price, which told Beck that she didn't have an unlimited budget. No surprise there. Faith had come from poor trash, and it'd no doubt taken her a while to climb out of that. She probably didn't have money to burn.

She made a soft sound that pulled his attention back to her. It was a faint groan. Correction, a moan. And for the first time since he'd seen her in the shower, there was a crack in that cool composure.

"I have to know if you're a real sheriff," she said, her voice trembling. "I have to know if it comes down to it that you'll protect my daughter."

Because the vulnerable voice had distracted him, it took him a second to realize she'd just insulted the hell out of him.

Beck stood and met her eye-to-eye. "This badge isn't decoration, Faith," he said, and he tapped the silver star clipped to his belt.

She just stared at him, apparently not convinced. "I want you to swear that you'll protect Aubrey."

Riled now, Beck walked closer. Actually, too close. No longer just eye-to-eye, they were practically toe-to-toe. "I. Swear. I'll. Protect. Aubrey." He'd meant for his tone to be dangerous. A warning for her to back down.

She didn't. "Good."

Faith actually sounded relieved, which riled him even more. Hell's bells. What kind of man did she think he was if he wouldn't do his job and protect a child?

Or Faith, for that matter?

And why did it suddenly feel as if he wanted to protect her?

Oh, yeah. He remembered. She was attractive, and mixed with all that sudden vulnerability, he was starting to feel, well, protective.

Among other things.

"Thank you," she added.

It was so sincere, he could feel it.

So were the tears that shimmered in her eyes. Sincere tears that she quickly blinked back. "For the record, I'm a good lawyer. And I'll be a good ADA." Now she dodged his gaze. "I have to succeed at this. For Aubrey. I want her to be proud of me, and I want to be proud of myself. I'll convince the people of this town that I'm not that same girl who tried to run away from her past."

She turned and waved him off, as if she didn't want him to respond to that. Good thing. Because Beck had no idea what to say. He preferred the angry woman who'd barked at him in the shower. He preferred the Faith that'd turned tail and run ten years ago.

This woman in front of him was going to be trouble.

His brother had once obviously been attracted to her. Beck could see why. Those eyes. That hair.

That mouth.

His body started to build a stupid fantasy about Faith's mouth when thankfully there was a rap at his door. Judging from Corey's raised eyebrow, he hadn't missed the way Beck had been looking at Faith.

"What?" Beck challenged.

Corey screwed up his mouth a moment to indicate

his displeasure. "I took a plaster of one of the foot-prints like you said. It's about a size ten. That's a little big for one of the Kendrick kids."

Beck had never believed this was a prank. Heck, he wasn't even sure it was a scare tactic. Those rocks had been meant to send Faith running, and Beck didn't think the killer was finished.

"I'll send the plaster and the two rocks to the Rangers lab in Austin tomorrow morning." With that, Corey walked away.

Realizing that he needed to put some distance be-tween him and Faith, Beck took a couple of steps away from her.

"My brother wears a size-ten shoe," Faith provided.

He stopped moving away and stared at her again. "So does your sister's ex, Nolan."

She blinked, apparently surprised he would know that particular detail.

"Even though the murders didn't happen here in my jurisdiction, I've been studying his case file," Beck explained.

Another blink. "I hope that means you're close to figuring out who killed my mother and sister."

"I've got it narrowed down just like you do." He shrugged. "You think it's Nolan. I think it's your brother, Darin, working with Nolan. The only other person I need to rule out is your daughter's father."

She folded her arms over her chest. Looked away. "He's not in the picture."

"So you said in your statement to the Rangers, but I have to be sure that he's not the one who put those rocks through the window."

"I'm sure he has no part in this," she snapped. "And that brings us back to Darin and Nolan. Darin really doesn't have a motive to come after me—"

"But he does," Beck interrupted. "It could be the house and the rest of what your mother owned."

Faith shook her head. "My mother disowned Darin four years ago. He can't inherit anything."

"Does your brother know that?"

"Darin knows." There was a lot emotion and old baggage that came with the admission. The disin- heritance had probably sparked a memorable family blowup. Beck would take her word for it that Darin had known he couldn't benefit financially from the murders.

"That leaves Nolan," Beck continued. "While you were on the phone, I did some checking. Your sister, Sherry, lived with Nolan for years, long enough for them to have a common-law marriage. And even though they hadn't cohabited in the eighteen months prior to her death, they never divorced. That means he'd legally be your mother's next of kin…if you and your daughter were out of the way."

Her eyes widened, and her arms uncrossed and dropped to her sides. "You think Nolan would kill me to inherit that rundown house?"

"Not just the house. It comes with three acres of land and any other assets your mother left. She only specified in her will that her belongings would go to her next of kin, with the exclusion of Darin."

"The land, the house and the furniture are worth a hundred thousand, tops," she pointed out.

"People have killed for a lot less. That's why I alerted every law-enforcement agency to pick up Nolan the moment he's spotted. I want him in custody so I can question him."

That caused her to chew on her bottom lip, and Beck wondered if she was ready to change her mind about staying in town. "I have to draw up my will ASAP. I can write it so that Nolan can't inherit a penny. And then I need to let him know that. That'll stop any attempts to kill me."

Maybe.

Unless there was a different reason for the murders.

The front door opened, and just like that, Faith raced out of his office and into the reception area. Corey was at the desk, by the dispatch phone, and Faith practically flew right past him to get to the three people who'd just stepped inside.

A Texas Ranger and a sixtysomething-year-old Hispanic woman carrying a baby in pink corduroy overalls and a long-sleeved lacy white shirt. Aubrey.

Faith pulled the little girl into her arms and gave her a tight hug. Aubrey giggled and bounced, the movement causing her mop of brunette hair to bounce as well.

Beck hadn't really known what to expect when it came to Faith's daughter, but he'd at least thought the child would be sleeping at this time of night. She wasn't. She was alert, smiling, and her brown eyes were the happiest eyes he'd ever seen.

"Sgt. Egan Caldwell," the Ranger introduced himself first to Beck and then to Faith.

"Sheriff Beck Tanner."

"Marita Dodd," the nanny supplied. Unlike the little girl, this woman's dark eyes showed stress, concern and even some fear. She was petite, barely five feet tall, and a hundred pounds, tops, but even with her demure size and sugar-white hair, she had an air of authority about her. "Aubrey's obviously got her second wind. Unlike the rest of us."

"Ms. Matthews," the Ranger said to Faith. "Could I have word with you?" He didn't add the word *alone,* but his tone certainly implied it.

"Of course." After another kiss on the cheek, Faith passed the child back to the nanny, and she and Sgt. Caldwell went to the other side of the reception area to have a whispered conversation.

Beck watched Faith's expression to see if she was about to get bad news, but if her brother had been caught or was dead, then why hadn't the Ranger told Beck as well? After all, Beck was assisting with the case.

"I really have to go the ladies' room," Marita Dodd said. That brought Beck's attention back to her.

"Down the hall, last room on the right," Beck instructed.

But Marita didn't go. She glanced at Aubrey, then at Faith, and finally thrust Aubrey in his direction. "Would you mind holding her a minute?"

Beck was sure his mouth dropped open. But if Marita noticed his stunned response, she didn't react. Aubrey reacted though. The little girl went right to him. Straight into his arms.

And then she did something else that stunned Beck.

Aubrey grinned and planted a warm, sloppy kiss on his cheek.

That rendered him speechless and cut his breath. Man. That baby kiss and giggle packed a punch. In that flash of a moment, he got it. He understood the whole parent thing and why men wanted to be fathers.

He got it, and he tried to push it aside.

This was the last child on earth to whom he should have an emotional response.

Aubrey babbled something he didn't understand and cocked her head to the side as if waiting for him to reply. She kept those doe eyes on him.

"I don't know," Beck finally answered.

That caused her to smile again, and she aimed her tiny fingers at the Ranger vehicle parked just outside the window. "Tar," she said as if that explained everything.

"Car?" Beck questioned, not sure what he was supposed to say.

"Tar," she repeated. Then added, "Bye-bye."

Another smile. Another kiss that left his cheek wet and smelling like baby's breath. And she wound her plump arms around his neck. The child obviously wasn't aware that he was a stranger at odds with her mother.

Beck was having a hard time remembering that, too.

Well, he was until he heard Faith storming his way. Her footsteps slapped against the hardwood floor. "Aubrey," she said, taking the child from his arms.

While Beck understood Faith's displeasure at having him hold her baby, Aubrey showed some displeasure, too.

"No, no, no," Aubrey protested and reached for Beck again. She waggled her fingers at him, a gesture that Beck thought might mean "come here."

"This won't take but another minute," the Ranger interjected. He obviously wasn't finished talking to Faith.

Faith huffed. Aubrey continued to struggle to get back to Beck, and she clamped her small but persistent hand onto the front of his shirt. They were still in the middle of the little battle when the phone rang. The deputy, Corey, answered it, but immediately passed the phone to Beck.

"It's your brother," Corey announced.

Great. This was not a conversation Beck wanted to have tonight.

Faith practically snapped to attention, and despite Aubrey's protest, she carried the child back across the room and resumed her conversation with the Ranger.

"Pete," Beck greeted his brother. "What can I do for you?"

"You can tell me if what I heard is true," Pete stated. "Is Faith Matthews back in town?"

Because he was going to need it, Beck took a deep breath. "She's here."

With that, Faith angled her eyes in his direction. Hearing his brother's voice and seeing Faith was a much-needed reminder of the past.

"Why did she come back?" Pete didn't ask in anger. There was more dread in his voice than anything else.

"She's the new assistant district attorney. I didn't tell you sooner because I didn't think she was coming until next month. It wasn't my decision to hire her. It was the DA's."

"It's for sure? The DA actually hired her?"

"Yeah. It's for sure."

"Then I'll have a chat with him," Pete insisted.

Beck had already had that chat, and the DA wouldn't budge. Pete wouldn't, either. His brother would talk and argue with the DA, too, but in the end the results would be the same—Faith would still be the new ADA.

"In the meantime, you do whatever it takes to get

Faith Matthews away from here," Pete continued. "I don't want her upsetting Nicole."

Nicole, Pete's wife of nearly a dozen years. This would definitely upset her. Nicole was what his grandmother would have called high-strung. An argument would give Nicole a migraine. A fender bender would send her running to her therapist over in Austin.

This would devastate her.

"There's a lot to be resolved," Beck told his brother.

"What does that mean?"

Heck, he was just going to say it even though he knew Faith would overhear it. "It means Faith might change her mind about staying."

Yeah, that earned him a glare from her. He hadn't expected anything less. But then she glared at whatever the Ranger said, too. Her glare was followed by a look of extreme shock. Wide eyes. Drained color from her cheeks. Her mouth trembled, and he wasn't thinking this was a fear reaction. More like anger.

"I'll call you back in the morning," Beck continued with his brother. "In the meantime, get some sleep."

"Right." With that final remark, Pete hung up.

Beck hung up, too, and braced himself for the next round of battle he was about to have with Faith. But when he saw her expression, he rethought that battle. No more shock. Something had taken the fight right out of her.

Sgt. Caldwell stopped talking to Faith and made his way back to Beck. "I got a call on the drive over here. The crime lab reviewed the surveillance disk you sent us. The one from Doolittle's convenience store. They were able to positively identify your suspect."

Beck let that sink in a moment. Across the room

while holding a babbling happy baby, Faith was obviously doing the same.

"So Darin Matthews was in LaMesa Springs?" Beck clarified.

The Ranger nodded. "We can also place him just five miles from here. About four hours ago, he filled up at a gas station on I-35."

Everything inside Beck went still. "Any reason he wasn't arrested?"

"The clerk thought Darin looked familiar, but he didn't make the connection with the wanted pictures in the newspaper until Darin had already driven away. But the store had auto security feeds to the company that monitors them, and that means we had fast access to the surveillance video. That's how we were able to make such a quick ID."

So Darin had come back, and he might have thrown those rocks with the threatening messages through Faith's window. "You didn't see Nolan Wheeler on either surveillance feed?" Beck asked.

"No. But that doesn't mean he wasn't there. He could have been out of camera range."

Beck snared Faith's gaze. "Does this mean you're leaving?"

She didn't jump to defend herself. Her mouth tightened, she kissed the top of Aubrey's head and looked at Sgt. Caldwell. "They want me to be bait."

Beck repeated that, certain he'd misunderstood. "Bait?"

"An enticement," the Ranger clarified. "We believe there's only one person who can get Darin Matthews to surrender peacefully, and that's his sister."

True. But Beck could see the Texas-size holes in this

so-called plan. "She's got a kid. Being bait isn't safe for either of them."

Sgt. Caldwell nodded. "We're going to minimize the risks."

"How?" Beck demanded.

"By making her brother think he can get to her. No matter where she goes, she'll be in danger. Her baby, too. My lieutenant thinks it's best if we make a stand. Here. Where we know Darin is."

Beck cursed under his breath, but he bit off the rest of the profanity when he realized Aubrey was smiling at him. "So what's the plan to keep her and that little girl safe?"

"The lieutenant wants to set up a trap to lure Darin back. We'll alert all the businesses in town and the surrounding area to be on the lookout for Matthews. Meanwhile, we'll put security measures in place for Ms. Matthews's house while she's at the hotel tonight."

"Her house?" Beck questioned. He didn't like anything about this plan. "You honestly expect her to stay there after what happened tonight? Someone threw rocks through her window."

Another nod. "She won't actually be staying at the house. She'll just make an appearance of sorts, but we'll tell everyone in town that's where she'll be staying."

Beck felt a little relief. "So Faith and her daughter will be going to a safe house?"

The sergeant glanced back at Faith, and it was she who continued. "Not exactly. I can't live in a safe house for the rest of my life, and Darin won't be able to find me if I'm hidden away. So the Rangers want to set up a secure place for Aubrey and the nanny. I'll be there, too, while making appearances at my house to coax out Darin. Obviously, we can't have Aubrey in harm's way, but my brother would know something was up if Aubrey's in one location and I'm in another. So we have to make it look as if she's with me even though she'll be far from danger." She paused, moistened her lips. "I'm hoping it won't take long for my brother to show, especially since he's already in the area."

So she agreed with this plan. But for someone in agreement, she certainly didn't seem pleased about it.

"If it weren't for Aubrey, I would have never gone along with this," she stated.

Confused, Beck shook his head. "Excuse me?"

"She means the protective custody issue," Sgt. Caldwell explained.

Beck sure didn't like the sound of this. "What about it? She doesn't want to be in the Rangers' protective custody?"

"No." Faith hesitated after her terse answer. "I don't want Aubrey to be in yours."

*"Mine?"* Beck felt as if someone had slugged him.

"Yours," Caldwell verified. "The Rangers will continue to provide you assistance on the case, but with a possible suspect in your jurisdiction, this is now your investigation, Sheriff Tanner."

"What are you saying exactly?"

The Ranger looked him straight in the eyes. "I'm saying we'll need your help. We can't risk it being leaked that Ms. Matthews really isn't staying at her place. And we can't keep her real whereabouts concealed if she's in the hotel for any length of time. There are too many employees there who could let it slip."

Beck's hands went on his hips. "So where do you propose her daughter and she go?"

"First, to the hotel to give us time to set up some security. Then, when everything's in place, they can go to your house. Her daughter will be in your protective custody." The Ranger didn't even hesitate.

It took Beck a moment to get his jaw unclenched so he could speak. "Let me get this straight. I'll become a bodyguard and babysitter in my own home?"

Sgt. Caldwell gave a crisp nod. "Protecting the child will be your primary task." The Ranger glanced at Faith again. Frowned. Then turned back to Beck. "Ms. Matthews has refused to be in your protective custody."

Her left eyebrow lifted a fraction when Beck's attention landed on her. "Yet you'd trust me with your daughter?" Beck asked.

"This wasn't her idea," Sgt. Caldwell interjected, though Faith had already opened her mouth to answer. "I had to convince her that this was the fastest and most efficient way to keep the child safe. And as for her not being in your protective custody, well, you can call it what you want, but it won't change what you have to do."

Beck stared at the Ranger. "And what exactly do I have to do?"

Sgt. Caldwell stared back. "Once we have this plan in place, Faith and her daughter's safety will be *your* responsibility."

## Chapter Four

This was not the homecoming Faith had planned.

From the window of the third-floor "VIP suite" of the Bluebonnet Hotel, she stared down at the town's equivalent of morning rush hour. Cars trickled along the two-lane Main Street flanked with refurbished antique streetlights. The sidewalks were busy but not exactly bustling as people walked past the rows of quaint shops and businesses. Many of the townsfolk stopped to say "Good morning."

There were lots of smiles.

She wanted to be part of what was going on below. She wanted to dive right into her new life. But instead she was stuck inside the hotel, waiting for "orders" from Beck and the Texas Rangers, while one of Beck's deputies guarded the door to make sure no one got in.

The three-room suite was a nice enough place with its soothing Southwest decor. Her and Aubrey's room was small but tastefully decorated with cool aqua walls and muted coral bedding. Marita's room was similar, just slightly smaller, and the shared sitting room had a functional, golden-pine desk and a Saltillo tile floor.

It reminded Faith of a gilded cage.

Of course, anything less than getting on with her new life would feel that way.

She forced herself to finish the now cold coffee that room service had delivered an hour earlier. She already had a pounding headache, and without the caffeine, it would only get worse. She had to be able to think clearly today.

What she really needed was a new plan.

Or a serious modification of the present one.

Aubrey was now in Beck's protective custody and he was responsible for her safety. Right. What was wrong with this picture?

She went back to the desk, sank down onto the chair and glanced at the notes she'd made earlier. It was her list of possible courses of action. Unfortunately, the list was short.

Option one: she could immediately leave LaMesa Springs, and go into hiding. But that would be no life for Aubrey. Besides, she had to work. She couldn't live off her savings for more than six months at most.

Faith crossed off option one.

Option two: she could arrange for a private body-guard. Again, that would eat into her savings, but it was a short-term solution that she would definitely consider. Plus, she knew someone in the business, and while things hadn't worked out personally between them, she hoped he could give her a good deal.

And then there was option three, and it would have to be paired with option two: try to speed up her brother's and Nolan's captures. The only problem was that other than making herself an even more obvious target, she wasn't sure how to do that. Maybe she could make an appeal on the local TV or radio stations? Or maybe she could just step foot inside her house a few times.

She already felt like a target anyway.

Frustrated, she set her coffee cup aside and grabbed a pen, hoping to add to the meager list. She sat, pen poised but unmoving over the paper, and she waited for inspiration to strike. It didn't.

The bedroom door opened, and Marita came out. Behind her toddled Aubrey, dressed in a pink eyelet lace dress, white leggings and black baby saddle oxfords. Just the sight of her instantly lightened Faith's mood.

"'i," Aubrey greeted her. It was her latest attempt at "hi" and she added a wave to it.

"Hi, yourself." Faith scooped her up in her arms and kissed her on the cheek.

"She ate every bite of her oatmeal," Marita reported. "And getting to bed so late doesn't seem to have bothered her." Marita patted her hand over a big yawn. "Wish I could say the same for my old bones."

"Yes. I'm sorry about that."

"Not your fault." Marita went to the window and looked out. "You warned me that some folks in this town wouldn't open their arms to you." She paused. "Guess Sheriff Tanner is one of those folks."

It wasn't a question, but Faith knew the woman wanted and deserved answers. After all, Marita had essentially been part of her family since Faith had hired her fifteen months ago as Aubrey's nanny. Faith had gotten Marita through an employment agency, but their short history together didn't diminish her feelings and respect for Marita.

"I left town ten years ago because of a scandal," Faith said, hoping she could get this out without emotion straining her voice. "Beck saw me coming out of a motel with his brother, Pete. His married brother. Word quickly got around, and his brother's wife attempted suicide because she was so distraught. Beck blames me for that."

Marita turned from the window, folded her arms over her chest and stared at Faith. "You *were* with the sheriff's married brother?"

Aubrey started to fuss when she spotted the stuffed armadillo on the settee, and Faith eased her to the floor so she could go after it.

"I was with him at the hotel." But Faith shook her head. She wasn't explaining this to Beck, who would challenge her every word. Marita would believe her. "But I didn't have sex with him. It didn't help that I couldn't tell the whole truth." She lowered her voice so that Aubrey wouldn't hear, even though she was much too young to understand. "It also didn't help that there were used condoms in the motel room. And when Beck found us, Pete was groping at me."

Marita made a sound of displeasure. "Beck was an idiot not to see what was really going on. You're not the sort to go after a married man." She glanced at the papers on the desk and frowned again. "Is that what I think it is?" Marita pointed to the document header, Last Will and Testament.

"I wrote it this morning." She noted the shocked look on Marita's face. "No, I'm not planning to die anytime soon. I just need to let someone know that he won't inherit anything in the event of my demise."

Faith didn't have time to explain that further because her cell phone rang. Since she was expecting several important calls, she answered it right away.

"Zack Henley," the caller identified himself. "I'm the driver who took you from the airport to LaMesa Springs last night. You left a message with my boss saying to call you, that it was important."

"It is. I need to know if you told anyone that you'd taken me to my house."

"Told anyone?" he repeated. He sounded not only surprised but cautious.

Faith rephrased it. "Is it possible that someone in LaMesa Springs learned that you had driven me to my house?"

He stayed quiet a moment. "I might have mentioned it to the guy at the convenience store."

That grabbed her attention. "Which guy and which convenience store?"

"Doolittle's, I think is the name of it."

The same store where her brother had been sighted. "And who did you tell about me?"

"I didn't tell, exactly. I mean, I didn't go in the place to blab about you, but the guy asked me what a cab driver was doing in LaMesa Springs, and I told him I'd dropped someone off on County Line Road. He asked who, and I told him. I knew your name because you paid with your credit card, and you didn't say anything about keeping it a secret."

No. She hadn't, but she also hadn't expected to be threatened with those tossed rocks. Or with the possibility that her brother had been the one to do the threatening. "Describe the person you spoke to."

"What's this all about?" he asked.

"Just describe him please." Faith used her courtroom voice, hoping it would save time.

"I don't remember how he looked, but he was the clerk behind the counter. A young kid. Maybe nineteen or twenty. Oh, yeah, and he had a snake tattoo on his neck."

She released the breath she didn't even know she'd been holding and jotted down the description. That wasn't a description of her brother. But it didn't mean this clerk hadn't said something to anyone else. Or her brother could have even been there, listening.

"Thank you," she told the cab driver.

Faith hung up and grabbed the Yellow Pages so she could find the number of the convenience store. She had to talk to that clerk. But before she could even locate the number, there was a knock at the door. Faith reached for her pepper spray, only to remind herself that there was a deputy outside and that a killer probably wouldn't knock first.

"It's me, Beck," the visitor called out.

Faith groaned, unlocked the door and opened it. It was Beck all right. Wearing jeans, a blue button-up and a walnut-colored, leather rodeo jacket. The jacket wasn't a fashion statement, though on him it could have been. It was as well-worn as his jeans and cowboy boots.

"My deputy needed a break," Beck explained. He didn't move closer until Aubrey came walking his way.

"'i," Aubrey said, grinning from ear to ear. It was

adorable. But in Faith's opinion that cuteness was aimed at the wrong person.

Beck, however, obviously wasn't able to resist that grin either because he smiled and stepped around Faith to come inside the suite.

"Is she ever in a bad mood?" he asked, keeping his focus on Aubrey.

"Wait 'til nap time," Marita volunteered. Unlike Aubrey's cheerfulness, Marita's voice had an unfriendly edge to it.

When Aubrey began to babble and show Beck the armadillo, he knelt down so that he'd be at her eye level. "That's a great-looking toy you got there."

"Dee-o," Aubrey explained, giving him her best attempt to say "armadillo." She put the toy right in Beck's face and didn't pull it back until he'd kissed it.

Aubrey giggled and threw her arms around Beck's neck as if she'd known him her entire life. The hug was brief, mere seconds, before she pulled back and pointed to the silver badge he had clipped to his belt.

"See?" Aubrey said. "Wanta see."

And much to Faith's surprise, Beck unclipped it and handed it to her so she could "see."

Frustrated with the friendly exchange, Faith shut the door with more force than necessary. Beck seemed to become aware of the awkward situation, and he stood.

"We need to talk," he told her, suddenly sounding very sherifflike.

That was obviously Marita's cue to give them some privacy, so she came across the room and picked up Aubrey. However, she stopped and looked at Beck.

"Maybe this time you'll be willing to see the truth," she snarled. She took the badge from Aubrey and handed it back to him.

"What does that mean?" Beck asked, volleying confused glances between Faith and Marita.

"Nothing," Faith said at the same time that Marita said, "She wasn't with your brother that night. Faith's not like that."

And with that declaration which would be hard to explain, Marita started walking. Aubrey waved and said, "Bye-bye," before the two disappeared into the bedroom.

"Don't ask," Faith warned him.

"Why not?"

"Because you won't believe me."

He lifted his shoulder. "What's not to believe? Didn't you tell me the truth ten years ago?"

"I told you I hadn't slept with your brother. That's the truth."

"He said otherwise."

She huffed and wondered why she was still trying to explain this all this time later. "Pete was drunk, and he lied, maybe because he was too drunk to know the truth. Or maybe because he didn't want you to know what'd really happened. I didn't seduce him, and I didn't take him to that motel. The only thing I tried to do was get him out of there."

Faith stopped when she noted his stony expression. "You know what? Enough of this. I don't owe you anything." To give herself a moment to calm down, she went to the desk and glanced at the notes she'd taken earlier. "I need to question a clerk at Doolittle's convenience store. The cabbie who drove me home told this clerk that I was in town. I want to find out who else knew so I can figure out who threw those rocks."

Beck just stared at her.

Unnerved and still riled, Faith continued, "You said we had something to discuss, and I don't think you meant personal stuff."

"Why would Pete lie about being with you?" He walked closer, stopping just a few inches away.

Why didn't he just drop this? "Ask him. For now, stick to business, *Sheriff*."

"The personal stuff between us keeps interfering with the business."

He caught her arm when she started to move away. Faith looked down at his grip, but he didn't let go of her. He kept those gunmetal-blue eyes nailed to her, and though she hadn't thought it possible, he got even closer. So close that she could smell coffee and sugar on his breath.

Faith hiked up her chin and met his gaze. "Be careful," she warned. She meant her voice to sound sharp and stern. It didn't quite work out that way.

Because something changed.

With his hand on her, with him so close, old feelings began to tug at her. She'd once been hotly attracted to him. A lifetime ago. But those years suddenly seemed to melt away.

She was still attracted to him. And this time, she didn't think it was one-sided.

She was toast.

"The Rangers installed some security equipment at your house," Beck said. His voice wasn't strained. Nor angry. He sounded confused, and the subject didn't fit the slow simmer in the air.

"Good," she managed to answer. She tried to step away, but he held on. And she didn't fight him.

She was obviously losing her mind.

"The Rangers dressed like security technicians so anyone looking wouldn't realize the authorities had staked out the place." He paused. His jaw muscles stirred. "There. That's what I came to say. Now, let's finish this." He shook his head. Cursed. Shook his head again. And finally, he let go of her and took a step back. "This can't happen between us."

"You're right. It can't."

Neither of them looked relieved.

And neither of them looked as if they believed it.

That tug inside her pulled harder. So hard that she moved away and returned to the window. She needed a few deep breaths before she could continue. "I want a different plan than the one the Rangers came up with."

He paused. Nodded. Nodded again. "I'm listening."

It took her a moment to realize that was all he was going to say. "Well, I don't *have* a different plan," she admitted. "I just *want* one."

"Welcome to the club. I sat up most of the night trying to make a list of options."

She huffed and glanced at her list. "Since Sgt. Caldwell made it clear that the Rangers don't have the manpower to provide protection for Aubrey, Marita and me, I was thinking of hiring a private bodyguard from Harland Securities in San Antonio. A friend owns the company."

"Ross Harland," Beck provided. "I've heard of him. He's your friend?"

"We used to date." Though she had no idea why she'd just told him that, especially since things hadn't ended that well between Ross and her. Ross might not even want to talk to her, but that wouldn't stop her from trying. "I plan to call him this morning and ask if he can help."

"You mean so that Aubrey and you won't be in my protective custody?"

Suddenly, that made her feel a little petty, but she pushed the uncomfortable feeling aside. Who cared if he was insulted that she would look elsewhere for protection? "You said yourself the personal stuff keeps getting in the way."

His jaw muscles went to war. "I swore I'd protect Aubrey, and I will. I'll protect you and Marita, too. There's not enough personal stuff in the world to ever stop me from doing my job."

She believed him. More than she wanted to.

Their eyes met again, and something circled around them. A weird intimacy. Something forged with all the emotion of the bad blood. And this bizarre attraction that had reared its hot, ugly head.

Faith forced herself to look away. To move. She shook off the Beck Tanner hypnotic effect and reached for the phone to call Ross Harland. She pressed in the number to his office, hoping she remembered it correctly, and the call went straight to voice mail. It was still before normal duty hours.

"Ross, this is Faith," she said. "Please call me. I'm in LaMesa Springs, and my cell-phone service is spotty so if you can't get through, you can reach me at the Bluebonnet Hotel."

She read off the number of the hotel phone and her

room number and clicked the end call button just as the door to the suite burst open. The movement felt violent. And suddenly so did the air around them.

The woman who rushed into the room was Nicole Tanner.

Beck's sister-in-law. Pete's wife.

Faith hadn't seen the woman since the night of the motel incident, but Nicole hadn't changed much. Sleek and polished in her high-end, boot-length, black duster, London blue pants and matching top. Her shoulder-length honey-blond hair was perfect. Not a strand out of place. She looked like the ideal trophy wife.

Except for her eyes and face.

The tears had cut their way through her makeup, leaving mascara-tinged streaks on her porcelain cheeks.

"Nicole, what are you doing here?" Beck demanded.

"Taking care of a problem I should have taken care of years ago."

And with that, Nicole took her hand from her coat pocket and aimed a slick, silver handgun right at Faith.

# Chapter Five

*Hell.*

That was Beck's first thought, right after the shock registered that his sister-in-law had obviously gone off the deep end. Now he had to diffuse this situation before it turned deadly.

Beck stepped in front of Faith. He didn't draw his weapon, though that was certainly standard procedure. Still, he couldn't do that to Nicole.

Not yet anyway.

He lifted his hands, palms out, in a backup gesture. "Nicole, put down that gun."

Nicole shook her head and swiped away her tears with her left hand. "I can't. I have to make her leave."

Beck could hear Faith's raw breath and knew she was afraid, but that didn't stop her from leaving the meager cover he'd provided her. She stepped out beside him.

"Get back," he warned her. "Nicole's not going to shoot me," he added. But he couldn't say the same about what she might do to Faith. He didn't want his sister-in-law to do anything stupid, and he didn't want bullets flying with Aubrey just in the next room.

He didn't want Faith hurt, either.

"I'm not leaving," Faith said, though her voice trembled slightly.

Man, it took courage to say that to an armed woman. Ill-timed courage.

"Let me handle this," he insisted. He then fastened his attention to Nicole. "You have to put the past behind you. Faith won't cause you any more trouble."

Nicole's hysteria increased. "She already has caused more trouble. Pete's been up all night talking about her. You know how he is when he gets upset. He shuts me out, and he drinks too much."

Beck did know. Like Nicole, Pete had a low tolerance for certain kinds of stress, and Faith's return would have set him off.

"Put down the gun, Nicole," Beck tried again. "And I'll talk to Pete."

"It won't do any good. I have to make Faith leave before it destroys my marriage."

"Your marriage?" Faith spat out. She obviously didn't intend to let him handle this in his own way. "You have a gun pointed at me, and my daughter is just one room away. You're endangering her as well as Beck, and yet your top priority is saving your marriage?"

Nicole blinked. She probably hadn't expected this. Faith hadn't stood up for herself ten years ago. "My marriage is in trouble because of you."

"No," Faith countered. "Your marriage is in trouble because of your cheating husband. Now, put down that gun, or I'll take it away from you myself."

Since this was quickly getting out of hand, Beck moved in front of Faith again. The new position wouldn't last long. Faith was already trying to maneuver herself to his side, but Beck didn't let that happen. It was a risk. He didn't want to push Nicole into doing something even more stupid.

"Give me the gun," he insisted. Beck didn't bolt toward her. He kept his footsteps even and unhurried. No sudden moves.

But Beck was just about a yard away when there was movement in the hall, just outside the suite. Nicole automatically glanced over her shoulder, and that split-second distraction was all Beck needed. He lunged at Nicole, snagged her by the wrist and latched on to the gun. The momentum sent them flying, and they landed against the two men who'd just arrived.

His brother, Pete, and his father, Roy.

"What the hell's going on here?" Pete shouted.

"I'm disarming your wife," Beck snarled. He took control of the gun and stepped back just in case anyone else decided to try to make a move toward Faith.

Pete shot Nicole a glance. Not of disapproval, either. The corner of his mouth actually lifted as if he were pleased that Nicole was in the process of committing a felony.

"I tried to get her to leave," Nicole volunteered.

"Well, this probably wasn't the way to go about it," her father-in-law interjected.

Good. Father was being reasonable about this. Beck needed another voice of support since Faith's and his didn't seem to be enough.

He checked Nicole's gun and discovered that it wasn't loaded. Beck showed Faith the empty chamber, causing her to groan again.

"I wanted to scare her into leaving," Nicole explained. "I didn't want to actually hurt her."

Well, that was something at least, but it didn't make this situation less volatile.

With emotion zinging through the air, his father and Pete stood side by side, and Pete glared at Faith. Roy only shook his head and mumbled something under his breath. The men were the same height, same weight, and with the exception of some threads of gray in Roy's hair, they looked enough alike to be brothers. That probably had something to do with the fact that Roy had only been eighteen years old when Pete was born.

Beck glanced back at Faith. He could tell she wasn't about to back down despite being outnumbered.

"Before this gets any worse, I want everyone to know that I'm not Beck right now. I'm *Sheriff* Tanner, and this is not going to get violent."

"Then she's leaving." That from Pete, and it was a threat aimed at Faith. Their father caught onto Pete's arm and stopped him from moving any closer.

"No. I'm not," Faith threatened right back. "Maybe it is time for an air clearing. For the truth. I'd planned to do it anyway, just not this soon."

That got everyone's attention, and the room fell silent.

Faith pointed to Pete. "I didn't sleep with you ten years ago. Or any other time."

There it was. The finale to the conversation that Faith and he were having shortly before Nicole arrived.

Beck pushed aside his own surprise and checked out the responses of the others. Nicole went still, the muscles in her arms going slack. The reactions of his father and brother, however, went in different directions.

Pete's face flushed with anger, and it seemed as if Father had been expecting her to say just that. He didn't look surprised at all.

"You were drunk," Faith reminded Pete. "All the years I've told myself that maybe you actually didn't lie about what happened, that you simply couldn't remember what you'd done, but now I'm not so sure."

"I didn't lie." Pete's voice was low and tight. Dangerous.

Faith walked closer. "Well, it wasn't me in that motel room with you. It was my sister, Sherry."

"Sherry," Beck mumbled. Since Sherry had been the town's wild child, he didn't have any trouble believing that, but apparently two members of his family did: Pete and Nicole. His father was still just standing there as if all of this was old news.

And maybe it was to him.

Had his father known the truth this whole time?

Nicole shook her head. "If that's true, why didn't you say so sooner? No one put a gag on you when you were outside the motel."

All attention turned back to Faith.

She pulled in a long breath. "I didn't say anything because Sherry's boyfriend, Nolan, would have killed her if he'd found out she cheated on him with your husband or with any other man, for that matter."

That made sense, and it also made Beck wonder why he hadn't thought of it sooner. But he knew why—he'd believed his brother.

"So why were you even there that night?" Nicole questioned Faith again. Judging from her expression, she wasn't buying any of Faith's account.

Faith took another breath. "When you came to the motel and started pounding on the door, Sherry called me. She was terrified word would get out that she'd been with Pete. I came over, hid on the side of the building and waited for you to leave. Then I took Sherry out of there. I was trying to get your husband out, too, when you and Beck showed up and accused me of seducing Pete."

"That's not the way I remember things," Pete insisted.

"Then your memory is wrong," Faith insisted right back.

Pete rammed his finger against his chest. "Why would I lie about which Matthews sister I'd slept with when I was drunk?"

"Only you can answer that, Pete." Faith volleyed glares at each one of them. "I want you all out of here. Now. If not, I intend to call the Texas Rangers and have you arrested."

He understood Faith's desire to be rid of his kin, but that riled Beck. Of course, he was already riled about this entire situation, so that was only frosting on the cake. "I don't need the Rangers to handle this," he assured Faith. "Do you want to file charges against Nicole?"

That earned him a fierce look from Pete, a raised eyebrow from his father and a surprised gasp from Nicole. Why, Beck didn't know. Nicole couldn't have possibly thought brandishing a gun, even an unloaded one, wouldn't warrant at least a consideration of arrest.

"I won't file charges at the moment," Faith said, pointing at Nicole. "But let's get something straight. I won't have you anywhere near my daughter or me with a weapon again. Understand?"

"But you ruined my life. *You.* It wasn't Sherry in that motel room. If it'd been your sister, my husband would have said so."

"Get them out of here," Faith mumbled, and she turned and walked into the adjoining room.

She didn't slam the door. She closed it gently. But Beck figured if she'd been wrongly accused and run out of town, that had to be eating away at her. Now add this latest incident with Nicole, and, oh, yeah, Faith was no doubt stewing.

"Go home, Nicole," Pete told his wife.

When Nicole didn't move, Roy caught onto his daughter-in-law's arm and led her toward the door. "I'm sorry about this, Beck. We'll talk later."

Beck nodded his thanks to his father and turned back to unfinished business. "Did you sleep with Faith or not?"

Pete glanced away. "What does it matter?"

Beck cursed under his breath. "That's not an answer to my question."

"Because it's not a question you should be asking. I'm your brother, for heaven's sake."

"Being my brother doesn't mean I'll gloss over your indiscretions. Especially if that indiscretion has put the blame on the wrong woman for all these years."

Pete looked him straight in the eye. "I was with Faith that night, not Sherry."

For the first time, Beck was seriously doubting that his brother had told the truth. But if he was lying, why? What could be worse than letting everyone, especially Nicole, believe he'd had sex with Faith? Unless fear of Nolan did play some part of this. The problem was his brother wasn't usually the sort to fear anyone.

"So what happens now?" Pete asked. "Faith just stays in town like nothing ever happened?"

Beck didn't want to mention that Faith, Aubrey and the nanny would soon be going to his house. And that they were in his protective custody. Besides, he didn't want anyone to know that his place was now essentially a safe house for the three. He wanted to get Faith, Aubrey and Marita in there without anyone else noticing. Or knowing about it. That would mean hiding them in the backseat of his car, parking in his garage and getting them inside only after the garage door was closed.

Of course, there was the other part to the plan. The part he could tell Pete since he needed the gossip mill working for the bait plan to succeed.

"Faith plans to stay at her mother's old house," Beck informed him, and he watched carefully for his brother's reaction. There wasn't much of one, just a slight shift in his posture. "I tried to talk her out of it, but she insisted on staying there."

"Then she's an idiot," Pete declared. "Her brother's a killer, and he's out on the loose. Anything could happen to her at that house."

And it wasn't a surprise that Pete didn't seem torn up about that. He probably wanted Darin to go after Faith.

Beck nodded and tried to appear detached from the situation. He realized, much to his disgust, that he wasn't detached. He didn't like this plan, and he didn't like that he'd just used his brother to set it into motion.

"You need to leave," Beck said, unable and unwilling to keep the anger from his voice. "See to your wife and make sure she doesn't come anywhere near Faith again."

Beck practically shoved his brother out the door, and he locked it. He made a mental note to keep it locked in case Nicole or Pete returned for round two. He needed to do some damage control from round one first.

Because once Faith gave it some thought, she just might file those charges against Nicole.

And if so, he'd have to arrest his own sister-in-law. Beck didn't want to speculate what kind of powder keg that would create between Pete, Nicole and Faith.

The phone on the desk rang. Figuring that Faith was still too shaken to answer it, Beck snatched it up. "Sheriff Tanner," he answered.

He was greeted with several seconds of silence, and for a moment Beck thought this might be another threat, similar to the rocks.

"Ross Harland," the caller finally said. "I'm returning Faith's call."

Beck glanced at the closed bedroom door. "She's, er, indisposed at the moment."

"Is she okay?" It didn't sound like a casual question, which might mean this guy, this former boyfriend, still had feelings for her.

"Faith's fine, but she had a rough morning. And a rough night, too."

"What happened?" Another noncasual question.

Beck didn't intend to get into specifics, but for anyone who knew Faith, her background was no doubt common knowledge. "Faith's brother is suspected of murder and is still at large. Aubrey and Faith might be in danger because of him."

"Who's Aubrey?"

That caused Beck to pause a moment. "Faith's daughter."

"A daughter?" He sounded shocked.

"I figured you knew."

"No. Faith and I dated for a year or so, but we stopped seeing each other nearly two years ago."

He didn't want to, but Beck quickly did the math. Aubrey was sixteen months old, which meant she'd been conceived a little over two years ago.

Right about the time Faith had been with Ross Harland.

Beck mentally groaned. Had Faith kept it from this man that he'd fathered a child?

"How can I help Faith?" Harland asked.

The question stunned Beck. Here, Beck had just told him in a roundabout way that he likely had a daughter, and Harland hadn't even asked about Aubrey. Certainly Harland could do the math as well. And that riled Beck to the core. If Aubrey had been his child, he'd sure as hell want to know, and he'd want to be part of her life.

"I'm not sure you can help," Beck answered, trying not to launch into a rant about how Harland should step up to the plate and be a man. "But Faith wanted to ask about getting a bodyguard for Aubrey."

Harland made a sound of understanding. "Well, I do have someone on staff who might work. Her name is Tracy Collier, and she's trained as both a nanny and a bodyguard. How old is Faith's daughter?"

Now the guy might finally get it. "Sixteen months."

"Good. I was hoping we weren't dealing with a newborn here."

"No. Not a newborn." Beck hesitated, wondering how much he should say and knowing he couldn't stop himself. He had to know, because despite Faith's denial, her past lover could have a part in this. "I thought you might be Aubrey's father."

"Me? Not a chance."

Beck had to hesitate again. This conversation was getting more and more confusing. "But you were with Faith about the time Aubrey was conceived."

"Look, I don't know what Faith told you about our relationship, and I'm not even sure it's any of your business, but there's no way that child could be mine."

"Birth control isn't always effective," Beck pointed out.

He cursed. "I want to talk to Faith."

"Like I said, she's indisposed. She'll have to call you back. And for the record, she never said you were Aubrey's father. I just put one and one together."

"Well, you came up with the wrong answer. Faith and I weren't lovers."

Beck nearly dropped the phone. "Not lovers? And you were together for a year?"

"Her choice. Not mine. Now, what the hell does this have to do with your investigation, Sheriff?"

Maybe nothing. Maybe everything. "Faith doesn't believe her brother is trying to kill her, and it's possible the danger is linked to someone in her past. When relationships go bad, situations can turn dangerous. Aubrey's father might have some part in this."

"Well, I don't know who he is, but he must be someone pretty damn special."

"What do you mean?"

Harland cursed again, and he stayed silent so long that Beck thought maybe the call had been dropped.

"Ask Faith why we never slept together," Harland finally said.

"Excuse me?" Beck said because he didn't know what else to say.

"You heard me. If you want answers, ask her." And with that, Harland hung up.

Beck glanced at the phone and then at Faith's bedroom door. He didn't know what the devil was going on, but he intended to find out.

# Chapter Six

"Beck Tanner asked you *what?*" Faith demanded.

There was a groan from the other end of her cell-phone line. "He thought I was your daughter's father," Harland explained.

Faith slowly got up from the bed where she'd been sitting and started to pace across the guest room in Beck's house. "What did you say?"

"The truth, that the child couldn't be mine because we were never lovers."

Faith didn't groan, but she squeezed her eyes shut a moment and silently cursed a blue streak.

"The sheriff said this was pertinent to the investigation," Ross added. "He said he wanted to be certain that none of your previous relationships could have a part in you being in danger."

"Maybe, but he had no right to ask you about our sex life." Or the lack thereof. Mercy, she did not want to explain this to Beck.

The truth could ultimately put Aubrey in danger.

"Anyway, the bodyguard I'm sending over is Tracy Collier," Ross continued, obviously opting for a less volatile subject. "She's one of my best. She should be there any minute, and she's yours for as long as you need her."

"Thanks, Ross," Faith managed to say. She did appreciate this, truly, but it was hard to be thankful when Beck might learn the truth.

"I'm sorry I told Sheriff Tanner anything about our relationship," Ross continued. "Should I phone him and have a little chat with him?"

It wouldn't be a chat. More like a tongue-lashing. "No. I'll do that myself." She thanked her old friend again and ended the call.

How dare Beck ask Ross a question like that, and he hadn't even had the nerve to tell her. But then he hadn't exactly had a chance, she reluctantly admitted. Like her, he'd been tied up all day planning to make Aubrey as safe as possible.

And they had succeeded. For now, anyway.

She, Marita and Aubrey were at Beck's house on the edge of town, and it appeared that no one had been aware of the move. Beck had literally sneaked them out the back of the hotel and into his place. Once the bodyguard arrived, then the plan was for a Texas Ranger to pull backup bodyguard duty while she and Beck made an appearance at her own house.

But first, she wanted to let Beck have it for that phone conversation with Ross.

Faith jerked open the guest-room door and stormed toward the family room, where she could hear voices. Beck's house was large, especially for a single guy: three bedrooms, three baths and an updated gourmet kitchen. A real surprise. When Beck had given them the whirlwind tour, she'd wanted to ask if he actually used the brick-encased, French stove or the gleaming, stainless cookware on the pot rack over the butcher's block island. But she hadn't said a word, because she hadn't wanted to intrude on his personal life.

He obviously hadn't felt the same about hers.

She nodded to Sgt. Sloan McKinney, a Texas Ranger who was sipping coffee while he stood by the kitchen door. Faith went straight to the family room and stopped dead in her tracks. Her temper didn't exactly go cold, but it did chill a bit when she saw what was going on. Marita was talking to a tall brunette. The bodyguard, no doubt. But it wasn't the bodyguard who snared her attention. Aubrey was on the floor, sitting in Beck's lap while he read *Chicka Chicka Boom Boom* to her.

Beck looked up at Faith, and his smile dissolved. Maybe because she looked angry. And was. And maybe because he knew the reason for her anger.

He'd changed clothes since they'd arrived and was now wearing black jeans and a white, button-up, long-sleeve shirt. Anything he could have worn would have made him look hot. But sitting there with Aubrey made him look hot and…extraordinary. It wasn't just his good looks now. It was that whole potential fatherhood thing. Beck seemed totally natural holding a child. Her child. And that created a bizarre ripple of emotions.

She had to remind herself to hang on to the anger.

"We'll go to your house when I'm done with the story," Beck let her know. Aubrey didn't take her eyes off the brightly colored pages.

"Faith, this is Tracy Collier," Marita said.

Faith shook the woman's hand. "Thank you for coming."

"No problem. Ross said it was important."

Yes, and Faith owed him for that. But not for what he'd volunteered to Beck.

"Sheriff Tanner checked my ID," Tracy volunteered. "And he ran a background check on me before I arrived." She didn't sound upset. More amused.

"She checked out clean," Beck informed Faith.

Though she was upset with him, she couldn't find fault with the extra security steps he'd taken with Tracy. But how could any man look that hot while jabbering nonsensical words like *chicka, chicka?*

Marita and Tracy resumed their conversation about sleeping arrangements. Apparently, Tracy had decided to take the sofa in the family room since it was near the front door. The Ranger would have a cot near the back door. Good. The arrangement gave Faith a little reassurance about leaving Aubrey, but it would still be tough.

Babbling, Aubrey tried to repeat the last line of the book that Beck read. He then did something else that shocked Faith. He brushed a kiss on Aubrey's forehead. There was genuine affection in his eyes. Aubrey's eyes, too.

Aubrey gave Beck a hug.

Beck's gaze met Faith's again, and he went from affection to a little discomfort. With Aubrey in his arms, he stood and walked to Faith.

"Ready to go to your house?" he asked.

No, but she was ready for that conversation. And ready to get her mind off Beck as a potential father.

Marita came to take Aubrey, and Faith gave the little girl a kiss. "Mommy won't be long."

Aubrey babbled something, reached for Beck again, but Marita moved her away. Faith gave her a nod of thanks.

"You don't want me reading to Aubrey," Beck mumbled.

"Yes. I mean, no." Since she was starting to feel petty again, she headed toward the garage. "I'm just surprised, that's all."

"Me, too. But it's hard not to get attached to her."

"Oh, that should make your family really happy," she snarled.

He didn't respond to that. They went into the garage, got into his SUV. Even though the windows were tinted and it was dusky dark outside, he still had her slip down low in the seat so that none of his neighbors, or a killer, would spot her coming out of his place.

On the backseat, there was a doll wrapped in a blanket. Faith already knew what she would do with that doll. She'd carry it into her house so that anyone watching would think it was Aubrey. The little detail had been Beck's idea because he said he didn't want anyone questioning why Faith wouldn't have her daughter with her at her house, especially since everyone in town likely knew about the child's arrival the night before.

Beck looked down at her. "You talked to Ross Harland," he said. Apparently, that was an invitation to start the argument he guessed they were about to have.

"You had no right to ask him those questions," Faith accused.

"I beg to differ. You don't think your brother is guilty. But I'm trying to figure out the identity of a killer. Your previous relationships are relevant." He pulled out of the garage and immediately hit the remote control clipped to his visor to shut it. He didn't pull away from the house until the door was fully closed.

Faith just sat there. Stewing. And waiting. She didn't have to wait long.

"Harland said he couldn't possibly be Aubrey's father," Beck continued. "I don't guess you intend to tell me who is."

"No." She didn't even have to think about her answer.

"That's what I figured you'd say, though I don't have a clue why you'd keep something like that a secret. I'm repeating myself here, but I'm trying to find a killer, Faith."

"And knowing Aubrey's father won't catch that killer."

He cursed under his breath. "I had a friend at the FBI fax me a copy of Aubrey's birth certificate. The father's name isn't listed. Just yours."

That had been intentional, and it would stay that way. Her silence must have let him know that because he didn't say anything else about it. Silently, he drove through LaMesa Springs and down Main Street—Faith could tell from the tops of the streetlights, but she was too low in the seat to actually see anything.

"No one seems to be following us," he explained, checking the rearview and side mirrors. He made the turn into the hotel and went to the back parking lot. Beck glanced all around them. "You can sit up now. I want people to think I picked you up here."

"But what if someone on the hotel staff blabs that I wasn't here all afternoon?"

"No one knows. There's been a Do Not Disturb sign

on the door and strict orders that no one goes into the room. Later, I'll phone the manager and tell him that I've moved you guys to your house."

Even though it was the plan, it still sent a chill over her. After that call, she'd officially be bait.

"So it was really Sherry in the motel with Pete?" Beck asked as he drove away from the parking lot. Except it didn't sound like a question.

But Faith answered it as if it'd been one. "What did your brother say?"

"He lied."

She glanced at him, and even in the darkness she had no trouble seeing his expression. A mixture of emotions. "How do you know that?"

"Because I could see it in his eyes."

Faith blew out a long breath. "Why didn't you see it ten years ago?"

"Because I wasn't looking. I just accepted what he told me as gospel."

"You accepted it because you already believed the worst about me."

He took a moment to answer. "Yes, and it's probably too little, too late, but I'm sorry."

She nearly laughed. For years, she'd wanted that apology. She'd wanted Beck to know the truth. But it seemed a hollow victory since she couldn't enjoy it. Well, not now anyway. But once the danger had passed it would no doubt sink in that this moment had been monumental.

Faith frowned.

She certainly hadn't expected an apology from Beck to feel so darn good. Maybe because she'd already written him off. She hoped it had nothing to do with this crazy attraction between them.

"I'll work on my father and Nicole," he continued, taking the final turn to her house. Even though the curtains all appeared to be closed, some lights were on. "Pete, too, eventually. Once they've accepted that you were the scapegoat in this, then your life here should be a little smoother."

"Thank you." That was a gift she certainly hadn't expected so soon. Then it hit her. "You're doing this for Aubrey."

"In part," he readily admitted. "I don't want her to feel any resentment from anyone. But I'm doing it for me, too. Because it's the right thing to do, and since Sherry is dead, I think this will help my family get past the hurt. You know that old saying—the truth will set you free."

"Not always," she said under her breath.

They came to a stop outside her house, directly in front of the porch. All she had to do was go up the steps, and she'd be inside.

Beck glanced at her again, and for a moment she thought he might have heard her and was going to question it. He didn't. He just looked at her.

He opened his mouth. Closed it. Shook his head. But he didn't explain why he was suddenly speechless. Instead, he picked up the doll, handed it to her and motioned for her to get out.

"Make it quick but not too obvious that you're trying to hurry," he instructed.

Faith did. While clutching the doll, she got out of the SUV and went inside to find Sgt. Caldwell waiting for them.

Beck and he exchanged handshakes. "Let's hope we catch a killer tonight," Beck greeted him.

"We'll do our best." The Ranger pointed to the security keypad by the door. "Before I leave, I want to go over the updates. There are external motion detectors that'll alert you if anyone comes within twenty feet of the house."

"What about windows?" Beck asked.

"All doors and windows are wired for security, and if anything's tripped, the alarm will go off, and the keypad will light up the problem area."

Faith was certain she looked confused. "But won't the alarm scare off Darin if he shows?" She propped the doll against the wall.

"No. The alarm will be a series of soft beeps. You shouldn't have any trouble hearing them, but they won't be loud enough to be heard from outside."

Beck's cell phone rang, and he stepped aside to answer it.

"The keypad's easy to work," Sgt. Caldwell continued. "Just press in the numbers one, two, three and four to arm it after I leave. Oh, and don't stand directly in front of any windows."

She had no plans for that. "If Darin shows, how fast can you respond?"

"Less than two minutes. I'll be nearby, parked several streets over. I don't want to be any closer, because if he sees me, it might scare him off."

"Two minutes," she repeated. "I hope that's fast enough to catch him."

Sgt. Caldwell lifted his shoulder. "Best case scenario is that your brother will call you first before he shows up. If that happens, just stay on the line with him and have Beck contact us so we can make a trace."

Faith nodded. "I don't want Darin hurt."

"We'll try our best. But it might not be possible. For that matter, it might not even be your brother who shows up."

"Nolan Wheeler," she provided.

Yes, he might have tossed those rocks through the window. And if so, if he was the one who arrived on her doorstep, then he could be arrested and questioned. It wouldn't tie up the loose ends with her brother, but she believed it would get a killer off the street.

Beck ended his call and rejoined them. One glance at him, and Faith knew something was wrong.

"That was the manager of the convenience store," Beck explained.

She held her breath, waiting for him to say her brother had been spotted again.

"Not Darin," Beck clarified, obviously understanding the concern in her body language. "This is about the taxi driver who stopped there after dropping you here at your house. When the clerk asked him what he was doing in LaMesa Springs, the driver told him."

Which confirmed what the taxi driver told Faith. "Let me guess—Nolan Wheeler was in the store?"

Beck shook his head. Paused. "No, but my father was."

"Your father?" she mumbled.

She didn't have to clarify what that meant. If his father knew, then so had Nicole and Pete. And after that stunt Nicole had pulled in her hotel room, Nicole could have been the one who'd thrown those rocks.

Beck looked away from her and handed Sgt. Caldwell his car keys. "I turned off the porch light. Figured it'd help in case someone's already watching the place."

And that person would believe it was Beck leaving. That's why Beck had changed his clothes, so that he would be dressed like the Ranger. Since no one knew the Ranger was there, the killer or her brother would think Faith was alone and vulnerable. Well, she wouldn't be alone, but the vulnerable part still applied.

"This could end up lasting all night," the Ranger reminded him.

Faith had considered that, briefly. What she hadn't considered was staying in the house alone with Beck. That suddenly didn't seem like a smart idea. But she couldn't let something like attraction get in the way of catching the person responsible.

"Good luck," Sgt. Caldwell said, heading for the door. He turned off the light in the entry as well and waited until Beck and Faith stepped into the shadows before he walked out. She immediately went to the door, locked it and set the security alarm.

"I'll talk to my dad," Beck promised. "I'll see if he repeated any information he got from the taxi driver. Plus, the rocks and foot casting are still at the crime lab. Either might give us some evidence."

"If it's Nicole who threw those rocks, I intend to file charges for that and the empty gun incident." Faith couldn't let the woman continue her harassment. Of course, if it was Nicole, there was a problem with the size-ten shoeprint that'd been found. Though maybe that print had been left earlier by someone not involved in this.

"If it's Nicole, I'll arrest her."

Faith caught his gaze. And saw the determination there. The pain, too. She also saw concern for her, so she thought it best if she stepped away from him.

Keeping in the shadows, she walked into the living room. Someone had taken the sheets from the furniture, and the sofa and recliner had a stack of bedding and pillows on them. This was where she and Beck were supposed to sleep. If sleep was even possible.

Beck would only be a few feet away from her.

With that overdue apology out of the way, there didn't seem to be so many old obstacles standing between them. Too bad. Because it made her remember a time when she'd lusted after him.

Who was she kidding?

She was still lusting after him. At least she was when she wasn't riled at him.

He followed her into the living room and caught onto her arm. The contact surprised her so much that she jumped. Faith reeled around, expecting him to do God knows what, but he merely repositioned her farther away from the window. He let go of her quickly, but then looked down at his hand as if that brief touch had caused him to feel something more.

"You might as well just go ahead and slap me," he said.

"For what?" she asked cautiously.

"For what I'm about to say."

Oh. With both curiosity and some fear, she considered the possibilities of what he might say. Maybe he wanted a discussion about the attraction. Or to discuss something about the touch that was still tingling her arm. Maybe he even intended to kiss her. Could that have been wishful thinking on her part?

"What?" she prompted when he didn't continue. Mercy. Her voice had way too much breath in it. She sounded like a lovesick schoolgirl.

"It has to do with the conversation I had with Ross Harland."

*Oh, that.* Faith hated that she'd anticipated anything not dealing with the case.

Beck moved closer to her again. Too close. "He was so adamant about not being Aubrey's father that I figured he was telling the truth about you two not having had sex." His voice was smooth and easy. No pressure, no expectations. He shrugged. "You can slap me for asking, and I doubt you'll answer, but at least tell me if Ross Harland might have anything to do with the murders."

That easy drawl took away some of the sting. "He doesn't."

He nodded. That was it. Beck's only reaction. He even seemed to believe her, which he should, since it was the truth.

The silence came. It was suddenly so quiet she could hear her own heartbeat in her ears. Seconds passed. Very slowly. While Beck and she just stood there and stared at each other.

"Is Ross Harland gay?" Beck finally asked.

She had no idea why that made her laugh, but it did. Maybe because Beck had lost the battle with curiosity after all. "No. He's not gay. And I don't know whether to be angry or flattered that you'd want to know so much about my sex life."

"Be flattered," he said, his voice all sex and sin.

She was. Flattered and suddenly very warm.

He leaned in, letting his mouth come very close to hers. Breath met breath. Her heart kicked into overdrive. So did her body.

She knew she should say something flippant and move away. But she didn't. "Beck," she warned.

But it sounded more like an invitation than anything else.

He didn't back away. Didn't heed her warning. He moved in for the kiss. His mouth brushed against hers. It was gentle. Nonthreatening. No demands.

It hit her like a boulder.

Faith felt the jolt. New sensations mixed with old ones that she thought she would never feel again. Leave it to Beck and his mouth to accomplish the impossible.

She leaned into him. Deepening the kiss with the pressure. He slid his hand around her neck, easing her closer. Inch by inch. Slowly, as if to give her a chance to escape. Beck was treating her like fine crystal.

And that kiss was melting her.

Faith heard herself moan. She felt the strength of his body. The fire was instant. The impact was so hard that she nearly lost her breath. She'd apparently already lost her mind. But then she broke the intimate contact and stepped back.

"I don't kiss a lot," she said, the words rushing out.

He cocked his head to the side. "Well, you should because you're good at it."

"No. I'm not." She didn't know what to do with her hands so she folded them over her chest.

His easy expression faded a bit. By degrees. Until it was replaced by confusion.

"I like to kiss," she clarified. Well, she liked to kiss

Beck, anyway. "But kissing leads to other things. Like sex. Which we aren't going to have."

He lifted his left eyebrow. "You're right. Our relationship is too complicated for sex."

"Yet you still kissed me."

He shook his head, cursed under his breath and dragged his hand through his hair. "I don't know why. Maybe because I haven't been able to get you out of my mind since I saw you naked in the shower. But I know that kiss can't go any further than it just did."

She blinked. "You honestly believe that?"

"I have to believe it. We can't deal with the alternative right now. Aubrey's safety has to come first. Then this investigation. Once we catch this killer, then we can…talk. Or kiss. Or do something we'll really regret like have great sex."

But he waved off that last part. Too bad she couldn't wave off the effect it had on her body. The image of them having sex sizzled through her.

"So *this* is on hold," he continued. "Unless there's something you want to tell me now."

She wanted to. But it wasn't that easy. The truth would give him some answers. More questions, too. And it would open Pandora's box.

Beck was right. Aubrey's safety came first.

Faith was about to repeat that, but a blast tore through the room.

## Chapter Seven

Someone had fired a shot at them.

The moment the sound of the bullet registered, Beck reacted.

He hooked his arm around Faith's waist and dragged her to the floor. She was already headed in that direction anyway, and they landed on the pile of sheets that'd been removed from the furniture. That cushioned their fall a little, but the new position didn't take them out of the line of fire.

Another bullet came at them and slammed into the wall just above their heads.

Hell.

Beck drew his weapon. "We have to move."

But where and how?

His initial assessment of the situation wasn't good. There'd been no broken glass, and that meant no broken windows. And no tripped motion detector, either. So the shooter had to be more than twenty feet away from the house and was literally shooting through the wall.

Probably with a high-powered rifle.

But it was the accuracy of the shot that caused Beck's

stomach to knot. Both bullets had come entirely too close, especially considering there was no way the shooter could have a visual on them.

. So, was the guy pinpointing them through some kind of eavesdropping device or had he managed to rig surveillance cameras that had given him an inside view of the house?

The third shot slammed into the wooden floor next to them and sent splinters flying. That was it. They couldn't stay there any longer.

"Let's go." Beck latched on to Faith's arm and got them running out of the living room. He needed to put another wall between them and the shooter.

Staying low, they raced toward the kitchen, the nearest room, but the shooter stayed in pursuit, and the bullets continued. Each blast followed them, tracking them as they made their way across the living room.

Beck shoved Faith ahead of him so that his body would give her some small measure of protection. It wasn't enough. They needed a barrier, something wide and thick. He spotted the fridge. It was outdated and fairly small, but he hoped the metal would hold back those bullets. He hauled Faith in front of it and shoved her to the linoleum floor.

The bullets didn't stop.

They tore through the kitchen drywall and shattered the tiny window over the kitchen sink. That set off the alarm, and the soft beeps began to pulse through the room. If the shooter moved to the back of the house, they'd be sitting ducks with that broken window.

"Call Sgt. Caldwell," Beck instructed Faith. He

handed her his cell phone and kept his gun ready just in case the shooter decided to bash through a window or door and try to come into the house.

Beside him, he felt Faith trembling, and her voice trembled, too, as she made the call to the Ranger and told him that someone was shooting at them from the front of the house. She asked him to come immediately.

Faith had no sooner made that request when the angle of the shots changed.

The next two rounds came right at the refrigerator. The bullets slammed into the metal but thankfully didn't exit out the front. The accuracy of the shots, however, told Beck that the gunman wasn't just using a high-powered, long-range rifle but that it was likely equipped with some kind of thermal scope or camera.

That thermal device could be a deadly addition.

It was no doubt picking up their body heat, and that heat had given away their exact location. That's why the shots were aimed so closely at them.

Faith ended her call with the Ranger. Even though the overhead light wasn't on, there was enough moonlight for Beck to see the terror on her face.

"Aubrey," she said, flipping open the phone again. She frantically stabbed in the numbers, and a moment later over the deafening blasts, she said, "Marita, is Aubrey okay?"

Beck hadn't been truly afraid until that moment. Faith was silent, and he watched her expression, praying that the gunfire had been only for them and a second shooter hadn't gone to his house to make a simultaneous attack there.

"They're fine," she finally said. Faith let out a hoarse sob. Fear mixed with relief.

Beck shared that relief. For just a moment. And then the anger took over. How dare this shooter put Faith through this. This was a blatant attempt to kill her, but the fear of harm to her child was far, far worse.

"I'll get this guy," Beck promised her.

The shots stopped.

Just like that, there were no more blasts. The only sounds were their sawing breaths, the hum of the central heating and the beeps from the security alarm.

"Is it over?" Faith asked.

He caught onto her arm to stop her from trying to get up. "Maybe."

Beck left it at that, but her widened eyes let him know that she understood. This could be a temporary cease-fire, a lure to draw them out away from the fridge.

Or it could mean the shooter was moving to the back of the house.

Where he'd have a direct shot to kill them.

"We'll stay put," he said, not at all sure of his decision. It was a gamble either way.

"I want to go to Aubrey," Faith mumbled.

"I know. So do I."

Waiting was hell, but this was the best way he knew to keep Faith alive.

His cell phone rang, the sound slicing through the room. Faith quickly answered it.

"Sgt. Caldwell's nearby," she relayed to him a moment later. "He'll turn on his sirens and an infrared scanner."

The sirens started to sound almost immediately. They would almost certainly scare off a shooter, if the shooter was still around, that is. But maybe, just maybe, the infrared would help Caldwell spot the shooter so he could be apprehended and arrested.

Beck wanted to be outside, to help with the search. He wanted to be the one to catch this piece of slime. But he couldn't leave Faith because the shooter could use that opportunity to go after her.

So he waited. It seemed endless. But it was probably only a couple of minutes before the phone rang again. This time, Beck grabbed it and answered it.

"It's Caldwell," the Ranger said.

"Did you get him?" Beck snapped.

"No. Nothing showed up on the infrared."

Beck groaned. This couldn't happen. They couldn't let this guy get away.

"I'm taking Faith back to my house to stay with the Ranger there and the bodyguard," he told the Ranger. "And then I'm going after this SOB."

FAITH CHECKED THE TIME on the screen of her cell phone. It was ten o'clock. Not that late, but Beck had been out looking for the shooter for well over an hour.

Each minute had seemed like an eternity.

She paced in the family room but kept her movements light so she wouldn't disturb Marita and Aubrey, who were already in bed and hopefully sleeping. Aubrey certainly was. Faith had verified that just five minutes earlier when she peeked in on them in the guest room. Marita had her eyes closed, but Faith doubted the woman was truly asleep.

The shooting had put them all on edge.

Tracy was on the sofa, reading. The Ranger, Sgt.

McKinney, was standing guard in the kitchen. Everything was quiet, but the tension was thick enough to taste.

*Where was Beck? And why hadn't he checked in?*

The silence was driving her crazy. She was imagining all sorts of things. Like he was lying somewhere shot. Or that he was being held hostage.

Because she was so caught up in those nightmarish thoughts, the sound of the phone ringing caused her to jump. "Hello?" Faith said as quickly as she could get the phone to her ear.

Silence.

That brought on some more horrible thoughts, and then she checked the caller ID. The person had blocked their number, and there was no reason for Beck to have done that.

"Who is this?" she asked.

Her alarmed tone obviously alerted Tracy, who got to her feet. She put her hand on the butt of the pistol that rested in her shoulder holster.

"It's me," the caller finally said.

Faith had no trouble recognizing that voice.

*Nolan Wheeler.*

Her stomach dropped to her knees from the shock of hearing him, but she welcomed this call. It was the first contact she'd had in years with a man she thought was a cold-blooded killer.

"Nolan," Faith said aloud so that Tracy would know what was going on. Tracy reacted. She went racing into the kitchen to tell Sgt. McKinney. Hopefully, they could do something to trace this call and pinpoint Nolan's location. "Did you take shots at me tonight?"

"Me? Of course not." He used his normal cocky tone,

but that didn't mean he was telling the truth. "I called about Sherry."

"What about her? She's dead. And I think you might be responsible."

"Not a chance. I didn't want her dead. She owed me money. Lots of it."

Faith was instantly skeptical. "How did that happen? You've never been one to have extra cash to lend anyone."

"I didn't exactly lend it to her. She stole my car and left a note, saying she was in a bind. She needed cash and needed it fast."

"Did she say why she needed money?" Faith asked.

"To gussy up." Nolan snickered. "Said she had to impress somebody, and she needed to look her best and that she'd pay me back. Killing her wouldn't get me the money so I've got no motive."

"What about the house? Did you think you could inherit it? Because you can't. I made a will, and there's no way you can ever inherit anything that's mine."

He made a tsk-tsk sound. "But I can inherit what's mine. Well, what was Sherry's anyway. Half of the place should have been hers after your mother was killed. Guess what, Faith? I want that half."

She fought to hang on to her temper. Flying off the handle now wouldn't solve anything. Besides, she wanted to give the Ranger more time to locate Nolan.

"Sherry and you separated eighteen months before her death," Faith reminded him. Even though their marriage was common law, Nolan probably did have a right to half of whatever Sherry owned. "And after the hell you put her through, you don't deserve anything from her estate."

"In the eyes of the law, I do. And you know the law, don't you?"

"I know it well enough that you won't see a penny."

"Oh, I want more than pennies," Nolan gloated. "A lot more. So here's the deal. You give me a hundred thousand dollars, and I'll go away."

*Oh, mercy.* "That's more than the place is worth, and besides, I don't have that kind of money."

"Then get it. Bye, Faith."

"Wait!" she said in a louder voice than she'd anticipated. This call couldn't end yet. "I need to know about Darin. Have you seen him?"

Nolan took his time answering. "He's around."

That was chilling, and despite the simple answer, it sounded like some kind of threat. "Where?"

"Don't worry about your brother. He can take care of himself."

"I'm not so sure of that, especially if you're manipulating him in some way." And if Nolan was in contact with her brother, then he was almost certainly manipulating him. "Where are you, Nolan?"

"Just get me that money," he said, ignoring her question.

Faith tried again. "Where are you?"

"I'm closer than you think, sweet cakes."

With that, Nolan hung up.

Faith looked in the doorway of the family room, where Tracy and the Ranger were standing. Sgt. McKinney took her phone and relayed the numbers to someone on the other end of his own cell-phone line.

A moment later, the sergeant shook his head. "The guy was using a prepaid cell phone. We couldn't trace it."

Faith didn't have time to groan because she heard the garage door open. Beck was home. And she raced to meet him. One look at his face, however, told her that he didn't have any better news than she did.

Beck took off his muddy cowboy boots and dropped them on the laundry-room floor. "I couldn't find the shooter."

Because he looked exhausted and beyond frustrated, Faith motioned for him to go into the family room so he could sit down. He smelled like the woods and sweat, and there were bits of dried leaves and twigs on his clothes.

"What about the shell casings?" Sgt. McKinney asked. "Caldwell called and said you'd found some at the scene."

"We did. They're Winchester ballistic silver tips." Beck looked at her. "They're used for long-range shooting. Coupled with what was probably a thermal camera or scope, I'm guessing the shooter had what we call a hog rifle. It's used for hunting wild hogs or boars at night."

"This type of weapon is rare?" she asked hopefully.

"Not around here. I know of at least a half dozen people who own one. Wild boars can be dangerous to people and livestock so they're usually hunted when they show up too close to the ranches."

Maybe Nolan had gotten his hands on one of these rifles. "Nolan Wheeler called a few minutes ago," she filled him in. "We couldn't trace the call."

The fatigue vanished. The concern returned. "What did he want?"

"Money. A hundred grand to be exact. He wants me

to give him more than half of my inheritance. But he didn't tell me how I could find him."

*I'm closer than you think.*

She pushed aside the chill from remembering Nolan's final remark. "He'll call back." Faith was certain of that. "He'll want that cash. And maybe we can use it to draw him out."

Beck hesitated a moment. Then nodded. "But you won't be the one who's drawing him out. No more playing bait."

Faith was still too shaky to argue with him. Nor did she argue when Beck reached out and pulled her closer. That was all it took. That bit of comfort. And Faith felt the tears well up in her eyes.

"I could use a cup of coffee," Tracy said, and she hitched her shoulder toward the kitchen. "Why don't you join me?" she asked Sgt. McKinney.

Faith didn't mind the obvious ploy to leave her and Beck alone because the tears started to spill down her cheeks.

"I'm sorry," she mumbled.

Beck pulled her even closer to him and closed his arms around her. She took everything he was offering her, even though it was wrong. Beck had been through that shooting, too, and he wasn't falling apart.

"I'm not ashamed of crying," she said, wiping away the tears with the back of her hand. Beck wiped away the other cheek. "But I wish I wasn't doing this in front of you."

"Why?" With his fingers still on tear-wiping duty, he caught her gaze, and the corner of his mouth hitched. "Because I'm the enemy?"

"No. Because you're Beckett Tanner."

The smile didn't fully materialize, and his fingers stayed in place. Warm on her cheek. "What would that have to do with it?"

"I always wanted to impress you. Or at least get your attention in a good way." She blamed the confession on the adrenaline crash and the fatigue.

"You succeeded. You got my attention. Even back then, before you left town." He slid his fingers down her cheek to her chin and lifted it slightly. As if he were readjusting it for a kiss. "You were about sixteen, and I saw you coming out of the grocery store on Main. You were wearing this short red dress. Trust me, I noticed."

Faith was stunned. "So why didn't you ask me out or something?"

"Because you were sixteen and I was twenty. The term *jailbait* comes to mind. I decided it'd be best to wait a couple of years."

For a moment, she got a glimpse of what life could have been if there hadn't been the incident at the motel. Of course, Beck's family would have never accepted her, and besides, the attraction would have run its youthful course and burned out.

She looked at him again.

Maybe not.

His mouth came to hers. Just a brush of his lips, and then he pulled back. When his gaze met hers again, the trip down memory lane was over. He drew her into his arms again. But it had nothing to do with kisses or sex. He eased her onto the sofa and simply held her.

For some reason, it seemed more intimate than a real kiss.

"I'm a good cop," he said, his voice hardly more than a whisper. "But I've made mistakes. I nearly let you get killed tonight."

So he was feeling guilty, too. "You couldn't have known that was going to happen."

"Yes, I did. I should have nixed that bait plan right from the start."

"It worked out all right," she assured him. Though they both knew that was a lie. They'd have nightmares about this for years. "I would just leave town, but I'm afraid this monster will follow me."

He made a sound of agreement.

Faith's phone rang again. She jolted. Her body was still on full alert. The caller had blocked the number.

"Nolan again," she mumbled. She answered the call and held the phone between Beck and her so he could hear as well.

"Hello, Faith."

It was a man all right. But not Nolan.

"Darin?" Though it wasn't a question. She knew it was her brother's voice. "God, I've been so worried about you. Where are you?"

"I can't say." He sounded genuinely sad about not being able to tell her that detail. "I called to warn you. You're in danger."

"Yes. From Nolan." She moved to the edge of the sofa. "I think he tried to kill me tonight."

"Maybe. But watch out for the Tanners. You can't trust them, Faith. They want to hurt you."

She wasn't exactly surprised after what had happened at the hotel. "Who, Nicole Tanner?"

"All of them. The whole family. If Sherry was alive,

she'd tell you the same. It's about those letters. Something went wrong with the letters."

Now she was surprised. "Darin, I don't understand—what letters? What do you mean?"

He stayed silent for several long moments. "Just be careful."

"Don't go," she said when she thought he was about to hang up. "I want to see you. Can we meet somewhere?"

That earned her a sharp look from Beck.

"No meeting," Darin insisted. "Not yet. It isn't safe. Not for you. Not for Aubrey."

"Aubrey?" Her breath practically froze in her throat.

Beck had a slightly different response. She saw the anger wash over him, and he tried to take the phone. She shook her head and eased her hand over the receiver. "He'll hang up if he knows you're listening," she mouthed.

"Aubrey's in danger because of the letters," Darin continued a moment later.

"Who has these letters?" Faith asked. "Nolan?"

"I don't know. Maybe."

If those letters contained something sinister, then Nolan was almost certainly involved. "Then I need to find him. Where is he?"

"He's here in LaMesa Springs."

*Here.*

*I'm closer than you think.*

And that meant Darin was probably in town, too.

"Yes, but where in LaMesa Springs?" Faith pressed.

"He's in the attic."

Faith flattened her hand over her chest to steady her heart. *Mercy, was Nolan here at Beck's house?* "What attic?" And she held her breath, waiting.

"At the house. Your house. He said the lock on the back door was broken so he went inside and climbed into the attic so he could wait for you. He got there before the cops and Rangers and then stayed quiet so they wouldn't hear him moving around."

"Darin?" Faith forced herself to talk. Nolan could be dealt with later. "I want to see you. Please."

But she was talking to herself. Her brother had already hung up.

Beck pulled out his own phone and jabbed in some numbers. Since the room was so quiet, Faith had no trouble hearing the man who answered. It was Sgt. Caldwell.

"Are you still at the Matthews house?" Beck asked the Ranger.

"Yeah. Why?"

"Check the attic. But be careful. One of our suspects, Nolan Wheeler, might be up there."

"I'll call you back," Caldwell let him know.

Beck hung up and looked at her. "Do you know anything about those letters Darin mentioned?"

She shook her head. This wasn't something she wanted to discuss right now. She wanted to know what was going on in that attic. But at least the conversation would keep her mind off the wait. Plus, this was important. "It sounded as if he believed they were connected to your family."

"Yeah, it did. But this is Darin, remember? He might not be mentally stable right now. Still," Beck continued before she could say anything, "I'll call my father in the morning and set up a meeting. I want to ask him about the convenience store anyway."

With everything else that was going on, she'd nearly forgotten about that. "I think it's pretty clear that he told Pete and maybe even Nicole that I was back in town. After all, your brother called you when I was still at your office. That was only a couple of hours after the rock throwing incident."

He mumbled another "yeah" and checked his watch.

"Sgt. Caldwell will be careful," she said more to herself than Beck.

But she prayed nothing went wrong and that the Ranger didn't get hurt. Besides, her brother could have been wrong. Beck was right about Darin possibly being delusional. God knows how much of what he said was real or a product of his mental illness.

Beck's phone rang, and he answered it immediately. He clicked on the speakerphone function.

"There's no one in the attic," Sgt. Caldwell explained. "But someone's been here. There's a discarded fast-food bag and graffiti."

"Kids maybe?" Beck asked.

"I don't think kids did this." His comment and tone upped the chill coursing through her. "I used my camera phone to take some pictures of the walls. I'm sending four of them to you now."

Beck went to the phone menu and pressed a few buttons. The first picture started to load on the screen.

Yes, it was definitely the attic. And though she couldn't see the fast-food bag the sergeant had described, she could see the wall that he'd captured in the photograph. Someone had taken red paint—at least she hoped it was paint—and written on the rough wood planks.

It was a calendar of sorts, crudely drawn squares, some blank, some with writing inside. The dates went back to a month earlier. She couldn't make out the writing and motioned for Beck to go to the next picture. It was the square with the date November 11th.

Inside the box someone had written:

Sherry dies.

Faith swallowed hard. That was indeed the day Sherry had been killed. But anyone who knew her sister would have had that information.

The next picture showed the date. November 12th. The caption inside:

Annie dies.

Her mother's name was Annie, and like the previous caption, it was correct. Her mother had been murdered then.

Picture three was dated January 12th with the words:

Faith's homecoming.

Yes, she had come home then. And someone had thrown rocks through her window.

God, had Nolan been there that whole time, waiting for her, watching her? The security had been set up to keep anyone from getting in, but what if he was already inside?

Beck clicked another button and the final picture loaded. There was a date: January 14th.

Tomorrow's date.

And beneath it were two words that caused her to gasp.

Faith dies.

## Chapter Eight

Faith was not going to die today.

Beck wouldn't let that happen.

It riled the hell out of him to think of the death threat that'd been left in her attic. It had shaken Faith to the core. Immediately after seeing those pictures on the phone, she'd sat motionless in his arms while he rattled off how he was going to put an end to this.

The handwriting and fast-food bag would be analyzed. That was a given. As would the shell casings collected from the attack the night before. But there was something else Beck could do. He could keep Faith away from her house. If he didn't let her out of his sight, he could protect her.

He hoped that'd be enough.

So, after giving her all the assurance he could, he'd sent her off to bed, where he was sure she hadn't gotten any sleep. He certainly hadn't. But that didn't matter. He could sleep later. Right now, he had to solve the case. The devil was in the details, and there was one detail he could further investigate.

He'd already called his father at the family ranch and

asked about the encounter with the taxi driver at the convenience store and the mysterious letters that Darin had mentioned to Faith. His father had become defensive, saying that it wasn't a good time to talk, but Beck didn't think it was his imagination that his dad was confused about those letters. Surprised, even. Maybe that meant his family had nothing to do with any potential evidence.

*Maybe.*

Since Pete and Nicole also lived on the grounds of the ranch, Beck would extend his questions to them and have that chat about giving Faith a much-needed break.

Beck got up from the kitchen table and poured himself another cup of coffee. He could hear the TV in the family room, where Tracy was having her breakfast. She was alone since the Ranger had left to assist with the processing of the crime scene at Faith's house. Beck had wanted to be part of that, but not at the expense of leaving Faith and Aubrey.

Before he could return to his seat and his case notes, he heard soft uneven footsteps. A moment later, Aubrey appeared. She was wearing a yellow corduroy dress and no shoes, just socks with lace at the tops.

She smiled and waved at him.

Just like that, the weight of the world seemed to leave his shoulders. "Good morning," he told her.

She babbled something with several syllables and went straight to him. "Up, up," she said.

Beck set his coffee aside and out of her reach, and he picked her up. Aubrey rewarded him with a hug and kiss on the cheek.

"She's faster than she used to be," Marita said, hurrying in. The nanny stopped and eyed them. "And she seems to think you're her new best friend."

There was worry in the woman's tone. Beck understood that. Faith had probably told her about their bitter past, but as far as Beck was concerned, that wasn't going to play a part in how he felt about his new best friend.

"Anything come back on that stuff you found in her attic?" Marita asked, helping herself to a cup of coffee. "Faith just told me about all of that while she was getting dressed."

So that's where she was. Beck had hoped she was still in bed. "We'll try to link the writing to Nolan Wheeler."

Marita flexed her eyebrows and had a sip of coffee. "Or Faith's brother."

Beck nodded and realized that Aubrey was studying him with those intense, cocoa-brown eyes. The little girl finally reached out and pinched his nose. She giggled. And Beck wondered how anyone could be in a bad mood around this child.

From the doorway, Faith stepped into view, studying him. She'd put on a pair of dark brown pants and a coppery top that was nearly the same color as her eyes. She'd pulled her shoulder-length hair into ponytail, a style that made him think of fashion models.

And kissing her neck.

He frowned, hating how he couldn't control those thoughts that kept popping into his head.

"I fixed some eggs," Beck let Marita and Faith know. He considered asking Faith how she was, but he knew the answer. Her eyes said it all. She was troubled and weary. Fear and adrenaline could do that.

Marita went to the stove and lifted the lid to a terra-cotta server. "This looks good. Really good."

"I put in a little smoked sausage and Asiago cheese." He got a little uncomfortable when both women stared at him. "I left some plain for Aubrey. If she can eat eggs, that is. I wasn't sure."

Great. Now he was babbling and sounding like a contestant on some cooking or parenting show.

Thankfully, Marita quit staring at him as if he had a third eye. She dished up some eggs and sampled them. "Mmm. A man who can cook. I think I'm in love," she joked.

"It's a hobby," Beck explained.

Faith smiled. An actual real smile. And that made all of his discomfort worth it. He wasn't embarrassed about his hobby, but it wasn't exactly something a man with his true Texas upbringing liked to brag about. Barbe-cuing steaks was one thing, but stove cooking and a cowboy image didn't always mesh.

It didn't take long, however, for Faith's smile to fade. "Anything new on the investigation?"

Yeah. And it was news she wasn't going to like. "There were no prints on the rocks and no match on the shoe impression. The sole was too worn to come up with anything distinguishable. Also, the track could have been there a day or two. It wasn't necessarily made by the rock thrower."

Faith stayed quiet, processing that information.

Aubrey pointed to the window, obviously wanting to go closer and look out, but Beck moved her farther away from it. The danger was just too great to do normal things, and if a gunman could shoot into Faith's house, he could do the same to Beck's if he found out Faith and Aubrey were there. He couldn't let that happen.

Marita dished up a small plate of plain eggs, took a spoon from the drawer and reached for Aubrey. "Why don't I feed this to her in the family room so you two can talk?"

When the nanny took Aubrey from him, Beck immediately felt the loss. So did Aubrey—her mouth tightened into a rosebud pout as Marita carted her away.

"You look…disappointed," Faith commented.

"I think being around Aubrey makes me think about being a father. I'm thirty-two. Guess this weird, gut feeling is the equivalent of my biological clock ticking."

Great. Now he was talking biological clocks after his cooking babble. He might have to go wrestle a longhorn to get back his manly image.

Faith lifted an eyebrow. "You want to be a father?"

Her astonished expression and tone stung. "You don't think I'd be a good dad?"

"No. I think you'd be very good at it." Faith walked closer and poured some coffee. She smelled like peach-scented shampoo. "I'm just a little surprised, that's all."

Another shrug. He tipped his head to the family room where he could hear Aubrey babbling. "What can I say? I've decided I want a child."

Actually, he wanted Aubrey.

Why did he feel such a strong connection to that little girl? Maybe because he was starting to feel a strong connection to Aubrey's mother.

Beck looked at Faith then, just as her gaze landed on him. Uh-oh. There it was again. The reminder of that kiss.

She moistened her lips, causing his midsection to clench. He had to move away from her, or he was going to kiss her again. But Faith beat him to it. She leaned in and brushed her mouth over his.

"Mmm," she mumbled. That sound went straight through him. "I shouldn't want you."

He smiled. God knows why. There wasn't anything to smile about. He was getting daddy fever, and he wanted Faith in his bed. Or on the floor.

Location was optional.

Because he was crazed with lust, Beck did something totally stupid. He hooked his arm around her waist and eased her to him. Body against body. It was a good fit. The heat just slid right through him.

"Does saying 'I shouldn't want you' make you want me less?" he asked, making sure it sounded like a joke.

"No." That wasn't a joking tone. A heavy sigh left her mouth. "It's complicated, Beck."

He was aware of that. But something was holding her back other than what'd happened in their past. "Want to tell me about it?"

He saw the hesitation in her eyes. "You'll want to sit down for this," she finally said.

Beck silently groaned. This sounded like trouble.

Before either of them could sit at the kitchen table, he heard the doorbell. It was almost immediately followed by a knock.

Beck snatched his gun from the top of the fridge. "Take Marita and Aubrey and go into the bedroom," he instructed.

Faith gave a shaky nod and started toward the family room. She didn't have to go far. Marita was carrying

Aubrey, and she was headed back into the kitchen. Tracy was right on their heels.

"Try to keep Aubrey quiet," Faith told them. She began to pick up the toys that'd been left in the room.

There was another ring of the doorbell. Another knock. Beck hurried to see who his impatient visitor was, but before he could get to the door, the key slid into the lock. He took aim. The door flew open.

His father was standing there.

Pete was behind him.

"Hell." Beck lowered his gun and cursed some more. His father had obviously not waited and used his emergency key to get in. "It's not a good time for a visit. We'll have to get together later."

His father eyed the gun. Then Beck. But Pete looked past Beck, and his attention landed on Faith. She had various toys clutched in her hands and was apparently headed to the bedroom. She froze.

"What's she doing here?" Pete demanded.

His father didn't let Beck answer, and he gave Pete a sharp warning look. "Maybe this is a good thing. She can probably clear up some of this mess."

Beck had no idea what *mess* his father was talking about, but he had a massive problem on his hands. His family now knew Faith's whereabouts, and unless he could convince them to keep quiet—and trust them to do so—then he was going to have to find a new location to use as a safe house. But he'd have to do that later. Right now, he needed to deal with the situation.

"What's this about?" Beck asked.

His father and brother stepped in and shut the door. "When you called earlier, you wanted to know if I knew anything about some letters that had to do with Sherry Matthews," Roy said. "Well, I do."

Beck was poleaxed. This was another unwanted surprise. Beck had expected his father to have no idea about that particular subject. "What do you mean?"

Roy pulled out a large manila envelope he had tucked beneath his arm. "These letters."

Beck placed his gun on top of the cabinet that housed the TV. Hoping this wasn't something that would lead to his father's arrest, he grabbed a Kleenex from the box on the end table, and he used a tissue so that he wouldn't get his prints on what might be evidence.

Still clutching the toys, Faith walked closer and watched as Beck took out the letters.

"Two and a half months ago, Sherry came out to the ranch to see Pete and me," Roy explained. "He wasn't there so I talked to her alone. She wanted money."

"Two and a half months ago?" Beck repeated. "That was just a couple of weeks before she was murdered."

"A week," Roy corrected. "She was very much alive when she left, but she said she was in big trouble. That she owed someone some money."

"Nolan," Faith supplied. "She called me about that same time, and I told her I couldn't lend her any more. I told her to work it out with Nolan."

"She didn't," Roy informed her. "Sherry said if Pete didn't give her ten grand in cash, then she was going to tell Nicole that she was having an affair with him. She said she'd tell Nicole she was having an affair with me, too."

Beck felt every muscle in his body go stiff. He waited for his father to deny it. He didn't. But Pete did.

"They were bald-faced lies," Pete volunteered.

"Sherry didn't wait around to say those lies to my face. She left, and a day later, the first letter arrived."

Roy nodded. "When I came out of the grocery store, it was tucked beneath the windshield wiper of my truck." He pointed to the letter in question.

The envelope simply had "Pete and Roy" written on it. No "to" or "from" address. Still using the tissue as a buffer, Beck took out the letter itself. One page. Typed. No handwritten signature. No date. No smudges or obvious fingerprints.

However, the envelope had obviously been sealed at one time, and since it was the old-fashioned, lick-and-press kind, he might be able to have that tested for DNA to prove if Sherry had indeed sent it. At this point, he had no reason to doubt that she was the sender, but it was standard procedure to test that sort of thing.

Not that his family had followed procedure.

They should have brought the letters to him, and maybe he could have prevented the murders.

"I need that money," Beck read aloud. "You two owe it to me, and if I don't have that ten thousand dollars by Friday, I'm calling Nicole. Miss Priss won't be happy to hear you're both sleeping with me again, and this time I have proof. Sherry."

*Again.*

That word really jumped out at him. Maybe it was a reference to the motel incident. Or maybe this was something more recent. If his brother could lie about the first, he could probably lie about the second. But where did that leave his father? Had he slept with Sherry, too?

"Sherry called after the first letter," Pete explained.

"I told her I wasn't going to give her a dime. The next day, the second letter was in the mailbox."

The second letter was typed like the first, but this one contained a copy of a grainy photo. It appeared to be Pete, sleeping, his chest bare and a sheet covering his lower body. Sherry was also in the shot, and it was a photo she'd obviously taken herself since Beck could see her thumb in the image. She was smiling as if she knew that this photo would be worth big bucks.

"That's not me in the picture," Pete insisted. "It's some guy she got who looks like me."

Maybe. It wasn't clear. It, too, would have to be tested and perhaps could be enhanced to get a better image.

"This is your last chance," Beck read aloud from the second letter. "If I don't have the money by tomorrow at six o'clock, a copy of this picture will go to Nicole. Leave the cash with my mom at the liquor store."

"When he got the second letter, I told Pete that maybe we should just pay Sherry off," his father explained. "I didn't care what people thought about me, but I just didn't want Nicole involved in this."

Since blackmailers were rarely satisfied with one payoff, Beck ignored that faulty reasoning and went on to the third letter. It was similar to the others, but this time Sherry demanded fifty thousand dollars, not ten. There was no copy of a photo, only the threat to spill all to Nicole.

"Why didn't you tell me about these letters before?" Beck asked.

"Because I wouldn't let him," Pete spoke up. "I wanted to handle it myself. And I didn't want anyone to know. I didn't want this to get back to Nicole. All it would have taken is for one of your deputies to let it slip, and this wouldn't have stayed private very long."

"I wouldn't have shown this to my deputies." His family must have known that was true, which made Pete's excuse sound even less plausible. But Beck couldn't doubt Pete's motives completely. He would have done anything to prevent Nicole from knowing. His brother might have a loose zipper, but he was obsessed enough with his wife that he would do anything to keep her from being hurt.

Pete pointed to Faith. "I think she was in on this blackmail scheme of her sister's. I think she knew all about it."

"I didn't," Faith said at the same moment that Beck said, "She didn't."

His comment got him stares from all three. "Faith's been up-front with me about this case. Unlike you two," Beck added. "You should have come forward with these and told me about Sherry's visit."

Not that it would have helped him catch the killer. But it would have given Beck the whole picture. Of course, it would have also made his brother and father suspects in Sherry's and her mother's murders.

Hell.

First that gun incident with Nicole. Now this. He might have to arrest a Tanner or two before this was over.

"Faith's brainwashed you," his father decided.

"That's not brainwashing," Pete piped in. "She's using her body to blur the lines. It's what the Matthews women are good at."

Beck slowly laid the letter aside and stared down his brother. "How do you know that?"

"What the hell does that mean?" Pete's nostrils flared. "Were you having an affair with Sherry?"

Pete cursed. "I won't dignify that with an answer."

"Why, because it's true?"

Roy caught onto Pete's arm when his son started to bolt toward Beck. "If your brother says he wasn't sleeping with that woman, then he wasn't."

The denial didn't answer the questions. "Then why would Sherry say it? Why would she have that picture? And why would she try to blackmail you?"

"Because she's a lying tramp, just like her sister." Pete jabbed his finger at Faith again.

That did it. Beck was tired of this. He put the letters aside, went to the door and opened it. "Both of you are leaving now. Once I've processed these letters, I'll let you know if I'm going to file any charges against you."

"Charges?" his father practically yelled. "For what, trying to be discreet? Trying to protect my family from a liar and schemer?"

Beck reminded himself that he was speaking to his father and tried to keep his voice level. "The Rangers could construe this as obstruction of justice."

Roy looked as if he'd slugged him. "Don't do this, son. Don't choose this woman over your own family."

"It's not about Faith. I'm the sheriff. It's my job to investigate all angles of a double murder." He ushered them out, closed the door and locked it.

Faith dropped Aubrey's toys onto the floor. She blew out a long breath and rubbed her hands against the sides of her pants. "I always say I'm not going to let your family get to me."

But they had. And Beck hated that.

Even though she had her chin high and was trying to look strong, Beck went to her and pulled her into his arms. He brushed a kiss on her forehead.

"I didn't know Sherry tried to blackmail Pete and Roy," she volunteered. "I didn't know anything about the letters until Darin mentioned them last night."

"I believe you. If you'd known, you would have told me."

He felt her go stiff, and she eased back to meet his gaze. She shook her head, and he got the sinking feeling that he was about to hear another confession that would cause his blood pressure to spike.

"I have to move Aubrey," she said. "Now that your father and brother know she's here, she can't stay."

She was right. Keeping Aubrey safe had to be at the top of their list.

He nodded. "I have a friend who's the sheriff over in Willow Ridge. I'll call him and see if he can set up a place for all of you there."

"No. Not me. I can't go with her. The danger is tied to me, not her. If I get her away from me, then she'll be safe. But if she stays with me, she could be hurt."

Beck wanted to shoot holes in that theory, but he couldn't. "Are you sure you can be away from her?"

"No. I'm not. I'll miss her. But I can't risk another shooting with her around." She blinked back tears. "You can trust this friend?"

"I can trust him," Beck assured her.

He let go of her so he could start making the necessary arrangements. Beck walked toward his office, and Faith went into the bedroom to tell the others that they'd be moving.

She was keeping something from him.

Damn it.

Here, he'd just blasted his family for withholding evidence and information. He'd given Faith a *carte blanche* approval when defending her. But she obviously had some kind of secret. Was it connected to the murders?

It must at least be connected to Sherry or Darin.

And that meant he'd have to deal with it as soon as he made arrangements for the safe house. He also needed to call the bank and find out if his father or brother had recently withdrawn a large sum of money. Beck hated to doubt them, but he had to think like a lawman.

It was possible that one of them had taken the cash to Sherry to pay her off. Maybe an argument had broken out. Maybe one of them had accidentally killed Sherry. Then maybe Sherry's mother had been killed because she suspected the truth. Or might she have been a witness to her daughter's murder?

Beck groaned and scrubbed his hand over his face. Oh, man. He hated to even consider that, but it was possible. He only hoped it didn't turn out to be the truth.

His phone rang, and when he checked the caller ID screen, he saw that it was from the sheriff's office.

"It's me, Corey," his deputy greeted him when Beck answered. "You're never going to guess who just showed up here at your office."

After the morning from Hades that he'd just had, Beck was almost afraid to ask. "Who?"

"Our murder suspect, Nolan Wheeler. And he's demanding to see you and Faith. Now."

# Chapter Nine

Faith could feel her heart breaking. Letting her daughter go was not what she wanted to do. She wanted Aubrey with her.

But more than that, she needed her child to be safe.

For that to happen, she had to say good-bye, even if it made her ache.

"It'll be okay," Beck assured her. Again. He'd been saying that and other reassuring things for the past three hours, since they'd started the preparations to move Aubrey and Marita to a safer location.

Faith wanted to believe him, especially since she didn't feel as if she had a choice. The killer had seen to that.

She kissed Aubrey again and strapped her into the car seat in Beck's SUV. Marita and Tracy were already seated, as was Sgt. Caldwell, who would be driving them to the sheriff's house in Willow Ridge. The Ranger had already promised her that he would take an indirect route to make sure no one followed. Every precaution would be taken. And he'd call her as soon as they arrived.

Faith's heart was still breaking.

Aubrey waved, first to Faith. Then to Beck, who was standing behind her. The little girl gave them both a grin, looked at Beck and said, "Dada."

Her words were crystal clear.

Faith stepped back and met Beck's gaze. "I have no idea why she said that."

He shrugged. "One of the books I read her yesterday had the word *daddy* in it. Guess she picked it up from there."

Relief washed through Faith. She didn't want Beck to think she'd coached Aubrey into saying that. Their lives were already complicated enough without adding those kind of feelings to the mix. But it was clear that her little girl was very fond of Beck.

Beck leaned in, kissed Aubrey's cheek. Faith added another kiss of her own, and Beck shut the door. They backed into the mudroom, and only then did the Ranger open the garage door.

Somehow, Faith managed not to cry when they drove away.

"We need to go to the station and deal with Nolan," Beck reminded her.

As much as she loathed the idea of seeing Nolan Wheeler, it'd get her mind off Aubrey, and would keep Nolan occupied while Aubrey was being transported to the new safe house.

"You don't have to see him," Beck said, heading toward the other vehicle, a police cruiser, that one of his deputies had driven over earlier. He had the manila envelope with Sherry's blackmail letters tucked beneath his arm, and he laid it on the console next to him. "You can wait in my office while I interrogate Nolan."

"Right," she mumbled. Faith got into the passenger's seat and strapped on the belt. "I'm doing this."

"You're sure?" Beck started the cruiser, drove out and closed the garage door behind him. "I told Corey to put Nolan in a holding cell and test him for gunshot residue. That was three hours ago. Nolan will be good and steamed by now that we didn't jump at his invitation to meet with him immediately."

Yes, but there was an upside to that. "With his short temper, maybe he'll be angry enough to tell us what we want to know."

And maybe that info would lead to an arrest. Preferably Nolan's. Faith wanted there to be enough physical evidence to prove Nolan had murdered her mother and sister. Then she could bring her little girl home and get on with her life.

Part of that included coming clean with Beck.

She needed to do that as soon as this meeting with Nolan was over and they had some downtime. She'd told Beck lies, both directly and by omission. He wouldn't appreciate that—it would put a wedge between them, just when they were starting to make some headway.

Faith touched her fingertips to her lips and remembered the earlier kiss. That kiss wasn't ordinary, but the truth was, it couldn't mean anything. It couldn't lead to something more serious. Still, she fantasized about the possibilities. What if all their problems were to magically disappear? And what if Beck could forgive her for lying to him?

Would they have a chance?

She silently cursed. She had enough on her plate without complicating things with a relationship.

"Having second thoughts?" Beck asked.

Faith looked at him. He glanced at her with those sizzling blue eyes and gave her a quick smile. He was very good with those smiles. They were part reassurance, all sex.

Wishing the attraction would go away wasn't working, and that meant she was fast on her way to a broken heart. She hadn't returned to town for that, but it seemed as inevitable as the white-hot attraction between them.

Beck pulled into a parking space directly in front of the back entrance to the sheriff's office. But he didn't reach for the door. He glanced around the parking lot before his eyes came back to her.

"I need to talk to you when we're done here," she said.

He stared at her, and for a moment she thought he was going to insist that conversation happen now. But he didn't. He glanced around the parking lot again and nodded. "Let's go inside. We'll talk later."

Beck ushered her into the break room and through the hall that led to the offices and the front reception.

Deputy Winston met them. "Glad you're here. Our *guest* is complaining."

"I'll bet he is," Beck commented. "What about the GSR test?"

"It was negative." Corey looked at her. "Probably means he wasn't the one who shot at you."

"Or it could mean he washed his hands in the past twelve hours," Beck disagreed.

Corey shrugged and hitched his thumb to the right. "I was watching the security camera and saw you drive up. I just took Nolan to the interview room. He's waiting for you."

Beck handed Corey the manila envelope. "I need you to process this as possible evidence in the Matthews murders. There are three letters inside. Use latex gloves when you handle them, then copy them and send the originals to the crime lab. I want the DNA analyzed and all the pages and envelopes processed for prints and trace."

Corey studied the envelope. "Where'd you get this?"

A muscle flickered in Beck's jaw. "My father and my brother. Once the letters are processed, I'll have them make official statements."

So there might be charges against his family members after all. Faith hated that Beck had to go through this and hated even more that she had to meet with Nolan. He wouldn't willingly give up anything that would incriminate himself. Still, a long shot was unfortunately their best shot.

Faith was familiar enough with the maze of rooms and offices that constituted the LaMesa Police Department. When she was sixteen, she'd had to come and pick up her mother after she'd been arrested for public intoxication. The holding cell had been in the center of the building, but this was Faith's first trip to the west corridor. The walls were stone-gray and bare, unlike Beck's office, which was dotted with colorful Texas landscapes, photos and books.

There were no books or photos in the interview room, either. Just more bare, gray walls and a heavy, metal table where Nolan was seated. Waiting for them.

Nolan stood when they entered, and Faith caught just a glimpse of his perturbed expression before it morphed into a cocky smile. The man hadn't changed a bit. His overly highlighted hair was too long, falling unevenly on his shoulders, and his stubble had gone several days past being fashionable. Ditto for his jeans, which were ripped at the knees and flecked with stains.

"You're looking good there, sweet cakes," he greeted her. Nolan's oily gaze slid over her, making her feel the urgent need to take a bath.

Faith didn't return his smile. "You're looking like the scum you are."

"Oh, come on." He pursed his mouth, bunched up his forehead and made a show of looking offended. "Is that any way to talk to your own brother-in-law?"

"My sister's abusive ex-live-in," she corrected. "You left a death threat for me in the attic of my house."

"It wasn't me. It was your brother." Nolan put his index finger near his right temple and made a circling motion. "Darin's loco."

Beck walked closer and stood slightly in front of her. Protecting her, again. Nolan didn't miss the little maneuver either. His cat green eyes lit up as if he'd witnessed something he might like to gossip about later.

"Have you two buried the hatchet?" Nolan asked.

"I rechecked your alibis for the nights of the murders," Beck said, ignoring Nolan's too-personal question. "They're weak."

Nolan shrugged and idly scraped his thumbnail over a loose patch of paint on the table. "I was at the Moonlight Bar in downtown Austin both times, nearly twenty miles from where Sherry lived. People saw me there."

"Yes, but those same people can't say exactly when you left. You had time to leave the Moonlight and get to both locations to commit both murders." Beck met him eye-to-eye. "So did you kill Sherry and Annie Matthews?"

"No." Nolan smiled again and sank back down onto the chair. "And you must believe that or I would have been arrested, not just detained."

"The day's not over," Beck grumbled. He pulled out a chair for Faith and one for himself. Both of them sat across from Nolan. "Where were you last night?"

"Any particular time that interests you?" Nolan countered.

"All night."

"Hmm. Well, I got up around noon, ate and watched some TV. Around six, I dropped by the Moonlight and hung out with some friends. I left around midnight."

Beck shook his head. "Can anyone confirm that?"

"Probably not." Nolan winked at her. "You really think I'd want to put a bullet in you? I've always liked you, Faith." Again, he combed that gaze over her.

The glare that Beck aimed at the man could have been classified as lethal. "I want your clothes bagged. My deputy will give you something else to wear."

Nolan lifted his left eyebrow. "And if I say no?"

"I'll make a phone call to Judge Reynolds and have a warrant here in ten minutes. Then I'll have you stripped and searched—thoroughly. Ever had a body cavity search, Nolan?"

For the first time since they'd walked into the room, Nolan actually looked uncomfortable.

"I also want a DNA sample," Beck added.

Faith felt her stomach tighten.

"Why?" Nolan challenged. "I heard there was no unidentified DNA at the crime scenes."

There wasn't, but there might be DNA in her attic. However, it wasn't the prospect of that match that was making her squirm.

"I want to make some DNA comparisons." Beck made it seem routine. "If you're innocent, you have nothing to worry about."

Nolan shifted in the chair. "Are you taking Darin's DNA and his clothes to test them for *comparisons?*"

"I would if I could find him."

"Maybe I can help you with that." Nolan let that hang in the air for several snail-crawling seconds. "He calls me a lot. And, no, you can't trace the number. He bought one of those cheapskate disposable phones. But when he calls again, I think I can talk him into meeting with you." Nolan was looking at her, not Beck, when he said that.

"If you believed you could arrange a meeting, then why haven't you already done it?" Faith asked.

"No good reason to."

"He's a murder suspect," Beck pointed out. "The police and the Rangers have been looking for Darin for two months."

"No skin off my nose." Nolan turned to her again. "But I'll do it. I'll set up a meeting, as a favor to you."

He probably thought this would make her more amicable about splitting the inheritance with him. And maybe she would be. If her brother was guilty. And if it got Darin off the street. But Faith wasn't at all convinced that Darin had committed these crimes.

"Set up the meeting if you can," Faith finally said. She stood. "Once I've talked with Darin, then and only then will I discuss anything else with you."

"Deal," Nolan readily agreed. "But one way or another, I'm getting that money. I don't care who I have to turn over to our cowboy cop friend here." Nolan flashed another smile before turning to Beck. "So am I free to go, after you get my clothes and my DNA?"

"Not just yet. Why don't you hang around for a while." It wasn't exactly a request.

Nolan's smile went south. "You can't hold me, Beckett Tanner. I got myself a lawyer, and she said there's not enough evidence for an arrest."

"Then I'll hold you here until your lawyer shows up," Beck informed him.

Faith didn't say anything until they were outside the room. "A good lawyer will have him out in just a few hours," she whispered.

"Well, that's a few hours that he won't be free to roam around and terrorize you." Beck walked to the reception, where Corey was waiting. "I want his clothes and his DNA, and I want it all sent to the crime lab ASAP."

"Will do. Are we locking him up?"

Beck nodded. "Until his lawyer shows. Maybe by then one of his alibis will fall through. The Rangers have put out feelers to see if anyone noticed Nolan leaving the bar in time to commit the murders. Or the shooting last night."

Corey grabbed an evidence kit from the supply cabinet behind him, and he strolled in the direction of the interview room.

Beck turned to Faith. "You really think Nolan can set up a meeting with your brother, or was that all hot air?"

"Maybe. Darin and Nolan aren't friends, but they did get along. Well, better than Nolan got along with the rest of us."

"Then maybe the meeting will pan out." Beck paused. "You flinched when I told Nolan I wanted a DNA sample."

"Did I?" Though she knew she had.

"You did." He blew out a deep breath and put his hands on his hips. "Nolan flirted with you in there. I thought there'd be more animosity. I thought I'd see more hatred in his eyes. But there wasn't any."

It took a moment for all that to sink in, and Faith was certain she flinched again. "What are you saying?"

But he didn't have time to answer. The front door flew open, and Nicole walked in. Faith automatically looked for a gun, but the woman appeared to be unarmed. Still, that didn't make this a welcome visit. She'd had more than enough of Beck's family today. Because of his father and brother's impromptu visit, Aubrey had had to go to a safe house.

"Her brother stole from me," Nicole announced.

That got Faith's attention, and she changed her mind about this visit. It might turn out to be a good thing. "You've seen Darin?"

But Nicole didn't answer her. Instead, she turned her attention to Beck. "That killer was at the ranch." She shuddered. "He was there and could have murdered us all."

"Let's go into my office," Beck suggested.

Faith silently agreed. Though they were the only ones in the reception area, it still wasn't the place to have a private discussion.

"I don't want to go into your office," Nicole insisted, and she wouldn't budge. "I want you to make her tell us where her creepy brother is so you can arrest him before he murders me like he did his mother and sister."

Beck held up his hands. "Faith doesn't know where Darin is. No one does. Now, what happened to make you think Darin wants to kill you, and what exactly did he steal?"

"He took a tranquilizer gun from the medical storage room in the birthing barn."

Faith pulled in her breath. A tranquilizer gun had been used to incapacitate both her mother and sister before they'd been strangled.

"I have proof," Nicole continued. She pulled a disk from her purse and slapped it onto the reception counter. "He's there, right on the security surveillance. He took it two and a half months ago, just days before the murders. He knew where it was because we've kept it in the same place for years, and as you well know, he used to work at the ranch part-time before all that mess at the motel."

*Oh, mercy.*

If this was true, it didn't sound good. Right up until the time of the murders, her brother had worked on and off as a delivery man for Doc Alderman, the town's only vet. The police had investigated the vet's supplies, but he could account for both of the tranquilizer guns in his inventory. Neither of those guns had prints or DNA from her brother. It was the bit of hope that Faith had clung to that Nolan had perhaps used a tranquilizer gun to set up Darin.

"And you just now noticed this tranquilizer gun was missing?" Faith asked.

Nicole still didn't look at her. She aimed her answer at Beck. "We haven't had to use it in ages. One of the ranch hands went in there to get it this morning to sedate one of the mares, and that's when we realized it was missing. Darin Matthews took it."

"That's on this disk?" Beck picked it up by the edges.

"It's there. It took me a while to find it. The security system in the storage room is motion-activated, and since the ranch hands hardly go in there, the disk wasn't full. I played it, and I saw Darin."

"You're sure it was him?" Beck asked before Faith could.

"Positive. You can see his face as clear as day."

"And you can see him take the tranquilizer gun?" Beck pressed.

Nicole dodged his gaze. "Not exactly. He moved in front of the camera, but what else would he have been doing in there?"

"Maybe delivering something for Dr. Alderman?" Faith immediately suggested. "Did you check with the vet to find out if he'd sent Darin out there to the ranch?"

"He had," Nicole said through clenched teeth. "Even though I'd told Alderman that I didn't want Darin anywhere near us."

"So maybe Darin was just delivering supplies," Beck concluded.

"Then what happened to the tranquilizer gun?"

"It could have been misplaced. Or someone else could have stolen it."

Anger danced through Nicole's cool blue eyes. "You're standing up for her again."

"I'm standing up for the truth," Beck corrected.

Her perfectly manicured index finger landed against his chest. "You're standing up for the Matthews family. I don't understand why. You know what they've done to us. The cheating, the lies."

"Pete cheated that night, too," Beck countered.

The color drained from Nicole's face, and she dropped back a step. "I expected this from the likes of her. But not from you." And with that, Nicole turned on her heels and hurried out the door.

Faith stood there silently a moment and tried to hold on to her composure. "Thank you," she said to Beck.

He turned and faced her. But he seemed unmoved by her gratitude. "I'll look at this disk," he said, his words short and tight. "And if there's any hint that Darin or anyone else stole that gun, I'll send it to the crime lab."

She nodded. "I expected that. I never expected you to give my brother a free ride. If Darin's guilty, I'll do whatever's necessary to catch him, and I'll support your decision to arrest him."

He searched her eyes, as if trying to decide if she was telling him the truth. Then he motioned for her to follow him to his office.

Faith did, and her heartbeat sped up with each step. The moment he made it into his office, Beck turned around to face her again.

"After watching the way Nolan reacted to you, I need to know." But he didn't ask it right away. He waited a moment, with the tension thick between them. "Is Nolan Aubrey's father?"

There it was. The question she'd been dreading.

Well, one of them anyway.

"Is he Aubrey's father?" Beck demanded when she didn't answer.

Faith shook her head, stepped farther inside and shut the door. "Maybe."

"Maybe? Maybe!" That was all he said for several

seconds. Seconds that he spent drilling her with those intense and suddenly angry eyes. "You don't know who fathered your own child?"

"No, I don't."

Faith took a deep breath and braced herself for the inevitable fallout that would follow. "Because I'm not Aubrey's biological mother."

# Chapter Ten

Beck dropped into the chair behind his desk, squeezed his eyes shut and groaned.

"I know, I should have told you sooner," Faith said. "But I had my reasons for keeping it a secret."

He slowly opened his eyes and pegged her gaze. "I'm listening." Though he was almost positive he wouldn't like what he heard.

Faith sat first. She eased into the chair as if it were fragile and might break. "Sixteen months ago, Sherry showed up at my apartment in Oklahoma. I hadn't seen her in months, but she was pregnant and needed money. I gave her what cash I had, and when she left, I realized she'd stolen my wallet. It had my ID and driver's license in it."

Beck didn't say a word because he'd already guessed how this had played out.

"The following day when Sherry went into labor, she used my name when she admitted herself to the hospital. She even put my name on Aubrey's birth certificate. I didn't know," Faith quickly added. "Not until after she checked out of the hospital two days later. She broke into my apartment and left Aubrey and a letter on my bed."

"Hell," he mumbled. He had guessed the part about Sherry being the birth mom. But not this. "She left a newborn alone?"

Faith nodded and swallowed hard. "Aubrey was okay. Hungry, but okay. Needless to say, I was a little shaken when I realized what Sherry had done."

Beck leaned closer, staring at her from across the desk. "Why didn't you tell anyone?"

"Because of the letter Sherry left. I have it locked away in a safety deposit box in Oklahoma if you want to read it for yourself. But Sherry told me in the letter that Aubrey would be in danger if her birth father found out she existed. 'He'll kill her,' Sherry wrote. 'You have to protect her. You can't tell anyone or she'll die.'" Faith shuddered. "I believed Sherry."

Yeah. Beck bet she had. He would have, too.

"You covered for your sister, again, just like you did ten years ago outside the motel with Pete."

Faith nodded. "I had to protect Aubrey. I loved her from the moment I laid eyes on her."

He understood that, too.

Beck wanted to be angry with Faith. He hated being lied to. He hated that she hadn't trusted him with something this important. But if their situations had been reversed, he might have done the same thing. All he had to do was look at the things he'd done to protect his own family.

"I'm sorry I let you believe she was mine." Faith swiped away a tear that slid down her cheek. "But she is mine, in every way that counts."

He didn't want to deal with Aubrey's paternity just yet. But he had to find out if this was connected to the case.

"Nolan could be the father," Beck said more to himself than to Faith. "But if he knew, he would have already tried to use her to get money."

Faith mumbled an agreement. "Sherry told me she'd kept her pregnancy a secret. That no one knew, except our mother and Darin. She left Austin when she starting showing and stayed in Dallas until the day before she came to see me."

Beck wasn't sure he could take Sherry's account at face value, but something must have happened to make her want to hide the pregnancy and her child. Or maybe the woman simply didn't want to play mother and conned Faith with that sob story. It felt real.

"If Aubrey's father is someone other than Nolan, he hasn't made any contact with me," Faith continued. "And if he'd talked to Sherry, she probably would have let me know. She was so worried about him finding out about Aubrey."

Beck thought that through. If Aubrey's birth father was the person responsible for the attempt to kill Faith, then why had he shot at her? If he wanted something— money, for instance—then why hadn't he gotten in touch with her so he could blackmail her?

"I don't think this is connected to the case," she added, her voice practically a whisper now.

"Maybe not, but we need to know for sure."

She shook her head and looked more than a little alarmed. "How can we do that without endangering Aubrey?"

"Do you have something of hers that would have her DNA on it?"

She stood, and he could see the pulse pounding on her throat. "I have her hairbrush in my purse, but I don't want her DNA tested. I believed Sherry when she said Aubrey could be in danger."

"I'm taking that threat seriously, too. But we have to know who Aubrey's father is. He could have killed Sherry and your mother. We have to rule him out as a suspect. Or else find him and arrest him."

"I know." A moment later she repeated it, and the fear and frustration made her voice ragged. "Sherry often had affairs with married men."

"And one of those men might not want the world to know he has a child." Beck stood, too, and walked closer to her. "So here's what we do. I'll package the hairbrush myself so that no one, including my deputies, will see it. Then I'll seal it and send it to the lab in Austin. I'll ask them to compare the DNA to Nolan's. And to mine."

Her eyes widened. "Yours?"

He obviously needed to explain this. "I'll ask Sgt. Caldwell to give the results only to me. But I want him to leak information that he did some DNA testing and that I'm Aubrey's father."

"What?" Her eyes widened even more.

From the moment the idea had popped into his head, he figured she'd be shocked. Still, this was a solution. Time would tell if the solution was a successful one. "If everyone believes I'm Aubrey's father, that'll stop Nolan or anyone else from being concerned that they've produced an unwanted heir."

With her eyes still wide, she shook her head. "Beck,

this could backfire. What happens when your family finds out?"

Oh, they would find out. No way to get around that. "They won't be happy about it, but it doesn't matter. This will keep Aubrey safe."

He hoped.

But there was another reason he wanted his DNA compared to Aubrey's. Beck was positive he wasn't the little girl's biological father, but he couldn't say the same for his brother. Or even his own father.

If Aubrey was his niece or his half-sister, then the test would prove it.

And if Aubrey was the primary motive for murder, that might mean there was a killer in his family.

FROM WHERE IT LAY on the coffee table, Beck's cell phone softly beeped again. An indication that he had voice mail. He didn't get up from the sofa and check it. Didn't need to. He'd already looked at the caller ID and knew the voice mails were from his father and brother.

He did check his watch though. It'd been six hours since he told Sgt. McKinney to get out the word that Beck was Aubrey's father. To make the info flow a little faster, Beck had told his deputy, Corey, the same necessary lie. The Rangers knew the truth. Corey didn't. He hoped Corey had leaked the little bombshell all over town, especially since Beck hadn't said anything about keeping it a secret.

Those two calls wouldn't be the only attention he'd get from his family. If he didn't answer their calls, they'd drop by for a visit—maybe even tonight. This time though, Beck had put the slide lock on. His father wouldn't be able to just walk inside as he'd done that morning. He'd also set the security system so if anyone tried to get in through any of the doors, the alarm would sound. Hopefully no one in his family would be desperate enough to try to crawl through a window.

He glanced at the numbers he'd written down when the bank manager had called him just minutes earlier. It was one of two other calls that brought bad news. Beck wasn't sure what to do about the second, but as for the first, he needed to investigate the bank figures from his father's account. Those numbers added up to trouble. They were yet another piece of a puzzle that was starting to feel very disturbing.

"Mommy misses you so much," he heard Faith say.

She was sitting on one of the chairs in the family room, just a few feet from him, with her phone pressed to her ear. She had her fingers wound in her hair and was doing some frequent chewing on her bottom lip. She was obviously talking to Aubrey, and it was the third call she'd made since the Ranger, Marita, Tracy and Aubrey had arrived at the safe house.

It wouldn't be the last.

This separation was causing her a lot of grief. Grief that Beck felt as well. But this arrangement was necessary. And hopefully only temporary. Once he'd caught the killer, then Faith could bring Aubrey home.

Wherever home was.

He doubted she could go back to her house, not with the attic death calendar and the shooting incident.

Faith got up from the chair and made her way to him. She held out the phone. "I thought you'd want to tell Aubrey 'Good night.'"

He did, but Beck knew all of this was drawing him closer and closer to a child that he should be backing away from. He needed to stay distanced and objective.

But he took the phone anyway. "Hi, Aubrey," he told her.

She answered back with her usual "'i" and babbled something he didn't understand, but Beck didn't need to understand the baby words to know that Aubrey was confused. She was probably wondering why her mother wasn't there to tuck her into bed.

"Your mommy will be there soon," he added.

The next syllables he understood. She strung some Da-da-da's together. Such simple sounds. Sounds Aubrey didn't even comprehend, but they were powerful.

"Good night," he said and handed the phone back to Faith.

"Good night," she repeated to Aubrey. "I love you."

Faith hung up, stood there and blew out a long breath. "It's hard to be away from her."

Beck settled for a "yeah."

She put her phone on the coffee table next to his and then looked around as if she didn't know what to do with herself. "I cringe when I think of the prenatal care Sherry would have gotten when she was pregnant. She wouldn't have taken care of herself. But thankfully, Aubrey turned out just fine."

"You've done a good job with her. You're a good mother, Faith."

Her eyes came to his. "I'm sorry about lying to you. For what it's worth, I'd planned to tell you today."

He believed her. It riled him initially, but ultimately brought them closer.

Like now.

She stood there, just a few feet away, wearing dark jeans and a sapphire-blue stretch top, something she'd put on after showering when they'd returned from his office. Her hair was loose, falling in slight curls past her shoulder.

She looked like the answer to a few of his hot fantasies.

His body wanted him to act on the fantasies, to haul her onto his lap so he could kiss her hard and long. Of course, because this was his fantasy, the kiss would be just the beginning.

And all that energy would be misplaced because he needed to do everything to make sure there wasn't another attempt on her life.

Forcing his mind off her body, he picked up copies of the three blackmail letters and spread them out over the coffee table so that Faith could see them. "With everything else that's happened today, I haven't had a chance to go over these. They could be important."

She made a sound of agreement, sat down on the floor near his feet and picked up the first one. "I find it interesting that Sherry sent the letters to both your father and brother. By doing so, she implicates both, which means she could have had a recent affair with either of them."

"Or neither."

Faith didn't look offended by that. She stayed quiet a moment, apparently giving that some thought. "True, but then why would she think she could get money from them unless there'd been some kind of inappropriate relationship? Because Nicole hated Sherry so much and blamed her for her emotional problems, an affair with either would have upset her. Both Roy and Pete would have wanted to prevent Nicole from finding out."

She paused, and her gaze snapped to his. Her eyes widened. "The DNA tests," she said. "You wanted to compare Aubrey's DNA to yours so you'd know if Roy or Pete is Aubrey's father."

He nodded.

"Beck, this could be a nasty mess if one of them is."

He nodded again.

"Oh, mercy." She dropped the letter on the table and tunneled her hands through the sides of her hair again. "What happens if it's true, if one of them is a DNA match?"

"Then I'll deal with it." Which was his way of saying that he didn't know what he'd do. Still, he and Faith had to know the truth, and this was one way of getting it. DNA could also exclude his relatives and hone right in on Nolan.

Shaking her head, she leaped up from the floor. "I'm not giving up custody. I've raised Aubrey since birth. I love her—"

"You're not going to lose her," Beck promised, though he had no idea how he'd keep that promise. If necessary, he'd just continue the lie that he was Aubrey's father.

He felt as if he were anyway.

Because he was losing focus again, Beck forced himself to look at the letters. "The third letter is different from the other two," he continued.

It took her a moment to regain her composure, but then she glanced at all three letters. "Yes. Sherry asks for more money in the third one. Maybe because Nolan pressed her for more. Ironic, since his car was probably worth less than a thousand bucks. He would have tried to get everything he could from her, all the while threatening to go to the police to report her for car theft. With her priors, she would have gone to jail."

That made sense, but he wasn't sure that the rest of it did. "Why would Sherry have typed the letters, especially since she put her name on them, visited my father and told him what she wanted? These letters are physical evidence and prove attempted extortion."

Faith lifted her shoulder. "Who knows why Sherry did what she did. Maybe she thought she could bluff her way out of extortion charges if she was arrested. She could claim she didn't type the letters." Faith paused. "You think someone else did?"

Now it was Beck's turn to shrug. But he also stood so he could deliver this news when they were closer to eye level. "The bank manager called when you were on the phone with Aubrey. It took some doing, but he found that my father had taken money from his various investment accounts. A little here, a little there, but it all added up to ten grand."

She walked closer and stopped right in front of him. "That's the exact amount Sherry was demanding in the first two letters."

"Yes. And she might have gotten it." His father might have paid Sherry off. He'd deal with that later, after he'd put more of this together.

"But if your father gave her the money, then why the third letter?" Faith asked.

"My theory is that someone else might have continued the blackmailing scheme."

"You mean Nolan." She didn't hesitate.

Neither did he. "Or your brother. Or even your mother. All it would have taken is knowledge of Sherry's plan and a computer to type the letters."

She bobbed her head, took another deep breath. "Nolan could have done this, and when Sherry threatened to expose him, he could have killed her."

That's what Beck thought, too. Nolan could have killed Sherry's mother if the money had been left with her. She would have known Nolan had a part in the scheme.

Because he was watching her, he saw Faith go still. "Is Nolan still being held at the sheriff's office?"

Hell. He hated to tell her this. "No. His lawyer showed up, and he was released about a half hour ago."

"I see." The words were calm enough, but the emotion was there in her expression and in her body.

"If I can get just one person at the Moonlight Bar to say they saw Nolan leave early on any of the three nights in question, then I should have enough to ask the DA to take this to a grand jury."

"In the meantime, Nolan is a free man. And he might stay that way. There's enough reasonable doubt, especially with the security disk of Darin in that barn."

Her voice didn't crack. Her eyes didn't water. He didn't touch her, but he did move closer.

"Some homecoming," she mumbled. She tried to smile at him, but it turned into a stare that ran the gamut of emotions. "But at least we're on the same side."

Oh, yeah. And more. They'd moved from being enemies to being comrades. To being…something else that Beck knew he should avoid.

But he didn't.

When Faith stepped closer, he didn't step back. He

just watched her as she reached out and touched his arm lightly with the tip of her fingers.

"How badly would this screw things up?" she asked.

"Bad," he assured her.

She nodded. Didn't step back. She didn't take her caressing fingers from his arm.

"I'm not good at this." Her voice dropped to a silky whisper. "But I'll bet you are."

Beck couldn't help it. He smiled.

And reached for her.

## Chapter Eleven

Beck's mouth came to hers, and just like that, Faith melted. The intimate touch, the gentle I'm-in-control-here pressure of his lips. The heat. They all combined to create a kiss that went straight through her.

She couldn't move. Couldn't think. Couldn't breathe. The kiss claimed her, just as Beck did when he bent his arm around her waist and pulled her to him. The sweet assault continued, and Faith could only hang on for the ride.

Or so she thought.

But then he stopped and eased back just a bit. That's when Faith realized her heart was pumping as if she were starved for air. She blamed it on the intense heat Beck had created with his kiss.

"You need a minute to rethink this?" he asked.

Did she?

Beck stood there, waiting. Breathing hard as well. Looking at her.

Faith looked at him, too. At those sizzling blue eyes. At that strong, ruggedly hot face. And she looked at his body. Oh, his body. That was creating more firestorms inside her.

Because her right hand was already on his chest, she slid it lower and along the way felt his muscles respond. They jerked and jolted beneath her touch. It was amazing that she could do that to him.

Beck didn't touch her. He stood there with his intense eyes focused on her and his body heat sending out that musky male scent that aroused her almost as much as his kiss had done.

Her hand went lower, while their gazes stayed locked. A muscle flickered in his jaw. His heart was pounding. Hers, too. So much so that she wasn't sure if that was her own pulse in her fingertips or if it was Beck's.

When she made it to his stomach, she slipped her fingers inside the small gap between the buttons of his shirt and had the pleasure of touching his bare skin.

*You can do this,* she told herself. She wanted to do this.

"You still need time to think?" Beck asked her. She was surprised he could speak with his jaw clenched that tight.

"No." She eased her fingers deeper inside his shirt, loosening a button until it came undone. "I don't need any more time."

Before the last syllable left her mouth, he kissed her. It was hard and hungry. If it hadn't fueled the need inside her, it would have been overwhelming. Suddenly, she wanted to be overwhelmed. She wanted everything she knew Beck was capable of giving her.

With their bodies still facing each other, he scooped her up in his arms. Faith wrapped her legs around him, and he immediately started toward his bedroom. They bumped into some furniture along the way. And a wall. Neither of them were willing to break the kiss so they could actually see where they were going.

Beck used his foot to shove open the door. The room was dark, with only the moonlight filtering through the blinds and thin curtain.

Several steps later, Faith felt herself floating downward. Her back landed against his mattress. And Beck landed against her with his sex touching hers through the barrier of their jeans.

She didn't want any barriers. She kicked off her shoes and went after his shirt.

Beck went after hers, stripping it over her head and tossing it onto the floor.

Everything became urgent. Frantic. A battle against time. She cursed her fumbling fingers but then gave a sigh of pleasure when she got his shirt off and put her hands on him. He was all sinew and muscle. All man.

And for the moment, he was hers for the taking.

So Faith took.

She kissed his chest and explored some of those muscles. Not for long though. Beck had other ideas. He unhooked the clasp of her bra, and her breasts spilled out. He fastened his mouth onto her left nipple and sent her flying.

*Mercy,* was all she could think.

He kept kissing her breasts and lightly nipped her with his teeth; all the while he worked to get her jeans off. She worked to get his off, too, though she had to keep stopping to catch her breath.

Her jeans surrendered and landed somewhere on the floor where Beck tossed them. Faith shoved down his zipper. He shoved down her panties. And for only a moment, she felt the cool air on the inside of her thighs.

The coolness didn't last.

Beck kissed her. The heat from his mouth warmed her all right and had her demanding that he do something about the fire he'd created inside her.

He stood and rid himself of his boots and jeans. She wished the light had been on so she could see him better, but the moonlight did some amazing things to his already amazing body. The man was perfect.

Beck reached in the nightstand drawer and pulled out a foil-wrapped condom. Safe sex. She was glad he'd remembered. She certainly hadn't.

He tugged off his boxers while he opened the condom. She got just a glimpse of him, huge and hard, before he came back to her, moving between her legs.

Faith forced herself not to think. She wanted this to happen. With Beck. Right here, right now.

Their eyes met. The tip of his erection touched her in the most intimate way and sent a spear of pleasure through her. She gasped and gasped again when he pushed deeper.

*Wow.*

With just that pressure, that movement, that sweet invasion, she was certain this was as much of the tangle of heat that she could take. She felt on the verge of unraveling.

But Beck stopped.

In fact, he froze.

Faith wanted no part of that. She hooked her leg around his lower back and shoved him forward.

There was a flash of pain. But it was quickly overshadowed by a flood of pleasure.

Beck didn't move. He stayed frozen.

She focused, trying to see his face, and the confused expression she saw there probably matched her own. He had questions.

"You're a virgin?" he asked.

Now it was her turn to freeze. "Sort of."

*Sort of? Sort of!* She wanted to kick herself for that stupid response. And she wanted to kick herself again because the moment was gone. Even though the need was still there, racing through her, she knew this wasn't going to continue until Beck got an explanation.

She caught onto him when he tried to move off her. "I tried to have sex with my boyfriend in college, but it didn't work out. I panicked."

"You're twenty-eight," he reminded her. This time, he did move off her. He landed on his back next to her and groaned. "There would have been other opportunities since college."

"One other, a few years ago. I panicked then, too." Faith hesitated, wondering how much she should say, but since she'd already messed this up, she went for broke. "When I was fourteen, one of Sherry's drunk boyfriends sneaked into my bedroom one night and tried to rape me. He didn't succeed, obviously. Darin came in and hit the guy with an alarm clock. Anyway, it took me a long time to get over that."

Beck cursed under his breath. "You're over it now?" he asked, staring up at the ceiling.

"I'm over it." Beck seemed to have cured her. Amazing that he could do what therapy hadn't.

He turned on his side and faced her. "Why didn't you tell me before I got you onto this bed?"

"I didn't want to explain what'd happened in my past. I wanted to have sex with you. And besides, I didn't think you'd notice."

"I noticed." It sounded as if he'd worked hard to keep the emotion and maybe even some sarcasm out of his voice. "Did I hurt you?"

"No." Since that sounded like a lie, she tried again. "Just a little, that's all."

This time the cursing didn't stay under his breath. "I'm sorry."

"No need to be. I'm not."

He stared at her, groaned and looked up at the ceiling again. "You just turned my life upside down. Now I've got positive proof that my brother's been lying all these years about what happened in the motel. And everything I'd ever thought about you was wrong."

"You thought I was a slut." She put her hand over his mouth so he wouldn't have to confirm that. "Everyone did. Because everyone believed I was just like my mother and Sherry. Guilt by association. But the truth is, I went in the opposite direction. I didn't want to be anything like either of them."

He stayed quiet a moment, before he reached for her and pulled her to him gently, and just held her.

"I never wanted to be any woman's first lover," he said. "It was sort of a badge of honor for some guys in high school. Not me. I figured it created some kind of permanent bond that I wasn't sure I wanted."

That stung a little. Was he saying he was sorry this had happened? Apparently. Because he wasn't doing anything to continue what they'd started.

"You don't owe me anything, Beck," she assured him.

"Oh, I owe you. An apology for starters for the way I've treated you." He kissed the top of her head. Cursed softly. And looked down at her. "What the hell am I going to do with you now?"

Though he probably didn't want her to answer, she considered pointing out that they were naked on his bed. But a soft thump stopped her from saying anything. The small sound came from the direction of the window. It sounded as if someone had bumped against the glass.

Beck shot off the bed.

"Get down on the floor," he told her.

Her heart banged against her rib cage, and Faith did as he said. Beck ran into the bathroom and seconds later emerged with his boxers on. He gathered up his jeans and started to put them on while he reached for something in his nightstand drawer.

A gun.

That got her moving.

She hurriedly crawled around, collected her clothes and got dressed. Once Beck had on his jeans, shirt and boots, he raced to the window. Pressing himself against the wall, he peered out the edge of the blinds.

"Hell, someone's out there," he let her know.

Her heart banged even harder. "Who is it?"

"Can't tell. He's dressed all in black, and he's crouched down near the rosemary bush in the side yard."

A ringing sound sliced through the silence. It was her cell phone. She'd left it in the family room.

"Stay put," Beck instructed. But a moment later, he cursed again. "The guy looks like he's trying to sneak away."

Oh, mercy. She didn't want him to get away. If it was Nolan, they could use this to arrest the man for trespassing. If he had a weapon, even better, because they could possibly charge him with criminal intent.

Beck started for the bedroom door. "My cell's not in here either. Use the phone by the bed and dial nine-one-one. Ask for backup. But I don't want sirens. I want a quiet approach so we don't scare this guy off."

She dialed the number as he asked. The dispatcher answered right away, and she relayed what Beck had told her. The dispatcher said he would send the night deputy immediately.

"Are you thinking about going out there?" she asked Beck the moment she hung up.

"I need to catch this guy," was his uneasy answer.

The silence lasted several seconds. "I have another gun on the top shelf in the closet," he instructed. "Get it and then stay low while you follow me to the back door. Lock it when I leave and set the security system. I won't be long."

"You don't know that. This guy could shoot you."

"I'm the sheriff," he reminded her. Plus, if he could end this tonight, then Aubrey wouldn't be in danger.

Her little girl could come back home.

"I'm doing this," Beck insisted.

Faith considered arguing with him, but she knew it would do no good. She hurried to the closet and took the .38 from the shelf. They crouched down and hurried to the back door.

"Be careful," she told him. But that was it. All she had time to say.

"Six-eight-eight-nine," he explained, disarming the

security system so it wouldn't go off when he made his exit. He shoved a set of keys into his jeans pocket. "Lock the door, reset it and then get back into the bedroom. Stay on the floor. I'll let myself back in when I'm finished."

And just like that, he hurried out.

Faith followed his instructions to a tee, added a prayer that he would be okay, and headed to the bedroom. She hadn't even made it there when the house phone rang. Five rings and the answering machine kicked in.

"Sheriff Beck Tanner," the machine announced. "I'm not here, so leave a message. If this is an emergency, hang up and call nine-one-one."

She waited, her mind more on Beck than the caller. And then she heard the voice.

"Faith?"

It was Darin.

She scrambled across the room and picked up the phone. "Darin, it's me. I'm here."

"I'm here, too. Outside Beck's house. I need to see you. I have something to show you."

Oh, God. Beck was out there expecting to catch a killer. He might shoot Darin by mistake. Of course, there was that possibility that Darin was the killer.

"I'm in the yard," Darin continued. "By some rose-bushes. There's a window nearby."

So he wasn't by the rosemary. He'd moved from the side yard to the back, where Beck had just exited. They'd probably just missed each other. She needed to tell Beck what was going on, but he didn't have his cell phone with him.

"I won't hurt you," Darin promised. And for a moment,

she remembered her brother, the one who'd saved her from Sherry's drunken boyfriend. The brother she loved.

With the cordless phone in one hand and the gun gripped in the other, Faith crawled back toward the kitchen. Toward the window with the roses.

"What do you need to show me?" she asked Darin.

"Sherry had some pictures of her with a man. I found them, and I think they're important."

It was likely the photo that Sherry had sent Pete and Roy, the one that proved she'd had the affair that might earn her some blackmail money.

When she reached the kitchen window, Faith lifted her head a little and looked out. She didn't spot her brother. "Darin, listen. Beck's out there, and if he sees you, he might shoot first and ask questions later. So I want you to stay put. Don't run. Don't make any sudden moves."

She saw something then. Was that a shadow in the shrubs or was it Beck?

She couldn't tell.

"Stay down," she told her brother in a whisper. She waited until Darin had gotten to the ground. Then she opened the window several inches, and in a slightly louder voice, she said, "Beck?"

Nothing. Not even from the other end of the phone, and she wondered if Darin had hung up.

Faith lifted the window a little more. The shadow didn't move. "Beck?" she called out.

She waited. Not long. Seconds, maybe. And a swishing sound came right at her. It happened in the blink of an eye.

Something tore through the mesh window screen.

There was a stab in her neck. Sharp and raw. But she didn't even have time to scream.

Faith felt herself falling, losing consciousness, and there was nothing she could do to stop it.

BECK STAYED CLOSE TO the house so he could use it for cover in case something went wrong and so he could make sure no one got inside to go after Faith.

The figure he'd seen in the yard might be a kid playing a stupid game, but with everything else that'd happened in the past two days, he couldn't take the chance. He also didn't want to leave Faith alone much longer, so that meant he had to find this guy and take care of the situation—fast.

He hoped it was Nolan so he could arrest him. Or beat him senseless, whichever came first.

Hurrying but keeping his gun aimed and ready, Beck went to the front of the house and looked around the corner. No one was there so he moved across the porch toward the side yard where he'd first seen the figure.

He silently cursed when he didn't see anyone there.

Had Nolan or Darin gotten away?

From up the street, he saw a cruiser approaching. The siren was off, but the deputy had his headlights on. He turned them off when he was about a half block away, parked the cruiser and got out. It was Deputy Mark Gafford. Beck motioned that he was going to go back around the house.

Beck stepped down from the porch and into the side yard where his bedroom extended to just a few feet from that rosemary bush. He glanced inside the bedroom window but couldn't see Faith. Good. That hopefully meant the killer couldn't see her either.

With the deputy now covering his back, Beck got moving again. Staying in the shadows. Keeping watch. He half expected someone to ambush him at any moment. Because after all, Sherry and her mother had been ambushed. But with each step, he heard nothing, saw nothing.

Until he made it to the backyard.

Someone was on the back porch at the door, dressed all in black. Could it be the same shadowy figure that'd been in the rosemary?

"Hold it right there!" Beck called out. He ducked partly behind the corner of the house to use it as cover in case the person fired.

But there was no shot.

The person bolted off the porch and began to run.

"Stop!" Beck yelled.

The guy didn't. Beck jumped on the porch in pursuit. From the corner of his eye, he saw Faith. On the kitchen floor.

His heart fell to his knees.

He called out her name, the sound ringing through his head, and he got a glimpse of the darkly clad figure rounding the corner, out of Beck's sight.

Beck didn't chase after him. Instead, he raced to the back door, forgetting that it was locked. God, he had to get to her.

There was blood on her neck.

"Watch out for a gunman," Beck yelled to his deputy, hoping the man would hear him.

He fumbled through his pocket for his keys. It seemed to take an eternity before he got the right one into the lock. Finally, it opened, and despite the fact he'd triggered the security system and it started to blare, he ran to her.

She wasn't moving.

Trying to keep watch to make sure the gunman didn't return, Beck pressed his fingers to the side of her neck that wasn't bleeding.

He felt her pulse. It was faint. But it was there. She was alive.

For now.

He reached up, yanked the wall phone from its cradle and jabbed in nine-one-one.

"Sheriff Tanner," he said, the second the dispatcher answered. "Get an ambulance out to my place now. Faith Matthews has been shot."

He tossed the phone aside and checked her injury to see what he could do to help her. She wasn't bleeding a lot, and he soon realized why.

The injury wasn't from a bullet.

Beck reached down and plucked the tiny dart from her neck. And he felt both relief.

And fear.

Because someone had shot her with a tranquilizer gun.

Just the way her sister and mother had been shot, right before someone had murdered them.

# Chapter Twelve

Faith forced her eyes open. No easy task, because her eyelids felt as heavy as lead. Actually, her entire body felt that way.

She glanced around and saw she was in a bed in a sterile white room. A hospital. That's when she remembered what had happened in Beck's kitchen.

Someone had shot her.

Her hand flew to her neck, to the thin bandage that was there. The skin beneath it was sore, but she wasn't actually in pain.

"Someone used a tranquilizer gun on you," a man said. "You're going to be okay." It was Beck. He was there. It was his voice she'd heard, and next to him stood Corey, his deputy.

"We didn't catch him," Beck added with a heavy, frustrated-sounding sigh.

"But you saved me. I didn't die," she mumbled.

Beck shook his head and walked closer. "You didn't die." His face was etched with worry, and judging from his bloodshot eyes, he hadn't slept in a while. Faith had no idea how long it might had been.

"How long have I been here?" she wanted to know.

Beck eased down on the side of the bed beside her and pushed her hair away from her face. His touch was gentle. "All night. It's nearly ten o'clock. There was enough tranquilizer in that dart to knock out someone twice your size. That's why you had to stay the night here in LaMesa Hospital."

"Ten o'clock?" That was too long. She had to find out who'd done this to her. She also had to check on Aubrey. Faith tried to get up, but Beck put his hand on her shoulder to make her lie back down.

"How are you feeling?" Corey asked.

So that it would speed things along and get her out of that bed, Faith did a quick assessment. Well, as quickly as her brain would allow. It felt as if her thoughts were traveling through mud. "I'm not in pain." She touched her throat and looked at Beck. "I guess you got to me before the killer could try to strangle me?"

"I got to you," Beck assured her, though that had not been easy for him to say. His jaw was tight again.

He was blaming himself for this.

Deciding to do something about that, Faith sat up. Beck tried to stop her again, but this time she succeeded. "How soon can I leave?"

He didn't look as if he wanted to answer that. "The doctor should be here any minute to talk to you."

She hoped he didn't hassle her about getting out of here. She wanted to get in touch with Marita and check on Aubrey. And her brother. She had to talk him into surrendering, or he was going to end up getting himself killed.

"Darin called me last night after you went outside,"

she explained to Beck. "He was there in your yard, but I don't think he's the one who shot me with the tranquilizer gun. I think someone else was out there."

Beck nodded. "There were two sets of tracks. I'm hoping I can match one of the sets to Nolan."

Good. That was a start and might finally lead to Nolan's arrest.

"I also had your neck photographed so the crime lab can compare your puncture wound to Sherry's and your mother's. The killer didn't leave the actual darts at those scenes so the lab can't make that comparison. But if the puncture wounds match, then we know the same person's responsible for all three attacks. Plus, they might be able to get some DNA from the dart I pulled from your neck."

And she prayed that DNA wouldn't belong to her brother. "Any sign of Darin or Nolan?"

Beck and Corey exchanged an uneasy glance. "No." Corey handed him an envelope that he'd been holding, and in turn Beck gave the envelope to her. "Darin left this by the rosebushes."

"Are these the pictures?" she asked, opening the envelope. "When he called last night, he said he had Sherry's pictures."

"And he obviously did," Corey mumbled. "I found them when I was processing the crime scene." He hitched his thumb toward the door. "I'll get back to the office and see if there's been any news about the case."

Faith waited until Corey was gone before she took out the first photograph. It was blurry and similar to the one in the blackmail letter. In the shot, there was a man lying asleep on a bed, and he was covered from the waist down with a white sheet. Maybe it was Pete, or even Roy, but it could have been Nolan with a wig.

In the second photo, someone had moved the sheet to expose the man's bare leg. Faith saw the spot on his thigh. A birthmark, she decided. She looked up at Beck for an explanation.

"Pete, my father and I all have that same birthmark."

Oh, no. Since she was dead certain that wasn't Beck in Sherry's bed, that left Roy and Pete. "The birthmark could be fake," she pointed out. "Nolan could have learned about the birthmark from Sherry and then painted it on to incriminate them."

Beck gave a crisp nod, an indication he'd already considered that. So why did he look as if that was a theory he didn't want to accept?

Faith tucked the second picture behind the third one. The last one. Again, it was a blurry shot, not of the man in the bed. This one was taken from long range, and it took Faith a moment to realize it wasn't Sherry.

It was a shot of her and Aubrey.

It'd been taken at the park about two months earlier. Right about the time the blackmail letters had been sent to Roy and Pete.

Faith drew in a sharp breath. "You think Sherry planned to use Aubrey to blackmail someone?"

But she didn't need an answer. She knew. This was exactly the kind of reckless thing Sherry would do.

"I have to go check on Aubrey," Faith insisted. She got out of the bed, and Beck looped his arm around her to steady her. If he hadn't, she would have fallen—her legs felt like pudding.

"Aubrey's fine," Beck assured her. "I talked to

Sheriff Whitley less than a half hour ago. No one has attempted to get into the safe house. You can't go check on her. It's too risky. Someone might try to follow you."

The disappointment was as strong as her concern for her daughter. But he was right. Faith couldn't take the danger to her child's doorstep. However, that didn't mean she had to stay put.

She was wearing a hospital gown, but Faith spotted her clothes draped over a chair. Wobbling a bit, she reached for the jeans and top.

Beck had her sit on the bed while he put on her jeans. It was a reminder that he'd done the exact opposite the night before when they were on his bed, and despite the hazy head and the punch of adrenaline, she remembered the heat they'd generated.

When she met Beck's gaze, she realized that he remembered it, too.

"Are you *really* okay?" he asked.

"I'm really okay." She was still wearing her bra, and he slipped off her gown and eased her stretchy blue top over her head so that she could put it on. "This wasn't your fault."

"Like hell it wasn't."

Because he looked as if he needed it, Faith put her arms around him. She would have done more. She would have kissed him for reassurance, both hers and his, if the door hadn't flown open.

*Pete and Roy.*

Apparently, there wasn't much security at the small-town hospital if anyone was allowed to march right into her room. That in itself was alarming enough. But her alarm skyrocketed when she spotted the blood on Roy's shirt. The man also had what appeared to be several fresh stitches on his forehead.

"Well, isn't this cozy?" Pete barked.

Faith stepped away from Beck as quickly as she could. But Beck didn't step away from her. He stood by her side and slipped his arm around her waist.

"What happened?" Beck asked his father.

Roy looked at her. "I had a run-in with your brother about a half hour ago."

Oh, God. "Are you hurt? Is Darin hurt?"

"My father's obviously hurt," Pete interjected before Roy could answer. "Darin is a sociopath and a killer."

"What happened?" Beck repeated, sounding very much like a cop now.

Unlike Pete, there was no anger in Roy's expression or body language. Just fatigue and spent adrenaline, something Faith could understand.

"I went out to the stables to check on a mare, and Darin was there," Roy explained. "He said he wanted to talk to me, but I didn't think that was a good idea. I grabbed my cell phone from my pocket to call you, and Darin tried to stop me." Roy lifted his shoulder. "I don't think he meant to hurt me. He just sort of lunged at me, and we both fell."

"Dad cut his head on a shovel and needed stitches," Pete supplied.

"What about Darin? What happened to him?" Beck wanted to know.

"He ran off, but I think he was hurt." Roy touched his wounded head and winced. "He was limping pretty badly."

As much as Faith hated to hear that, she hoped it would make Darin seek medical attention, and then maybe, finally, she could talk to him.

Roy looked at her. "I heard what happened to you. Could have been worse."

"Much worse," she supplied. "I'm sorry about what went on with my brother. He's scared, and he needs help."

"He needs to go back to the loony bin," Pete jabbed. "And maybe you do, too." But he didn't aim that last insult at her but rather Beck. "What's this I hear about you being the father of her kid?"

So the info had indeed been leaked, though it was ironic that the first question about it had come from Pete, the man who might very well be Aubrey's biological father. Faith didn't want to know what kind of problems that was going to create if he was. Of course, the alternatives were Roy and Nolan. Nolan was a jerk. Possibly even a killer. And Roy seemed too decent not to own up to fathering a child.

But then maybe Sherry hadn't told him.

"You didn't mention a word to us about the baby," Roy continued where Pete had left off. "Or about being with Faith."

"Because I knew you wouldn't approve." Not exactly a lie. They wouldn't have.

Pete's hands clenched into fists. "So you're saying it's true, that you are the kid's father?" But then he relaxed a bit. "Oh, wait. I get it. You slept with her on a down and dirty whim, and then she claimed you got her pregnant. And you actually believed her?"

Roy caught onto Pete's arm. "If Beck thinks the little girl is his, he must have a good reason to believe it."

"I do," Beck supplied. "I also have a good reason to believe that Pete lied ten years ago. You didn't sleep with Faith."

The anger flushed Pete's face. "You're taking her word over mine?"

"No. I'm taking what I know over what you said. I think you lied because you thought Nolan would pound you to dust if he found out you'd been with Sherry."

She expected Pete to return fire, but he didn't. He went still, and it seemed from his expression that he was giving it some thought. Several moments later, he scrubbed his hand over his face.

"I wasn't afraid of Nolan," Pete finally said. "And I don't remember what went on in that motel room."

Pete seemed to be on the brink of an apology, or at least an honest explanation, but Beck's cell phone rang. Pete shook his head again, and she could tell that he'd changed his mind about saying anything else.

"What?" Beck snapped at the caller.

That got everyone's attention. So did Beck's intensity. He cursed and slapped the phone shut.

"That was Nicole," he explained. "She said she just found a dead body in the west barn at the ranch."

BECK CAUGHT ONTO FAITH'S arm to stop her from bolting from the cruiser when he brought it to a stop in front of the west barn at his family's ranch.

"I have to see if it's Darin," she insisted.

Not that she needed to tell him that. From the moment he'd relayed Nicole's message, Faith had been terrified that the body belonged to her brother.

Beck figured it did, but he didn't say that to her.

Still, he couldn't discount the altercation Darin had had with Roy just an hour or so earlier. His father had even said that Darin was injured. Maybe he'd hit his head, and that had caused his death.

That wouldn't make it any easier for Faith to accept.

This was going to hurt, and Beck wasn't sure she would let him help pick up the pieces.

Nicole was there, standing in front of the dark red barn, waiting. There wasn't a drop of color in her face, despite the cold wind whipping at her.

"I have to go in first," he instructed Faith. He drew his weapon, just in case. "I have to do my job."

He didn't wait for her to acknowledge that. Behind him, Pete and Roy pulled up. And behind them was Corey. All three men barreled from their vehicles.

Beck got out and held out his hands to stop them from going any farther. "Corey, I need you to wait here with Faith. Pete and Dad, you wait with Nicole. As soon as I've checked it out, I'll let you know what's going on."

None of them argued, maybe because none of them were anxious to have a close encounter with a dead body.

"I couldn't see his face," Nicole volunteered. "But it's a man, and he's dead in the back stall. There's blood, a lot of it," she added in a hoarse whisper.

Pete pulled her into his arms, and Beck gave Corey one last glance to make sure he was guarding Faith. He was. So Beck went inside.

The overhead lights were on, so he had no problem seeing. The barn was nearly empty, except for a paint gelding in the first stall. He snorted when Beck moved past him. Beck walked slowly, checking on all sides of him.

With the exception of six stalls and a tack room at the back, there weren't many places a killer could hide.

If there was a killer anywhere around.

But Beck figured Darin would be the only person he'd find inside. That meant he'd have to interview his father about the fight he had with the man, and Beck only hoped that he had told the truth. He didn't want to find out his father had shot an unarmed man.

Beck spotted a pair of boots sticking out from the back stall. Judging from the angle, the guy was on his back. He wasn't moving, and there was a dark shiny pool of blood extending out from his torso. Nicole had been right—there was a lot of it. Too much for the person to have survived.

Keeping his gun ready and aimed, Beck went closer. There was a piece of paper on the open stall door. The top of the page was slightly torn where it'd been pushed against a raised nail head that was now holding it in place. Beck decided he would see what that was all about later, but first he needed to ID the body and determine if this person was truly dead or in need of an ambulance.

More blood was on the front of the man's shirt. And in his lifeless right hand, there was a .38. The barrel of the gun was aimed directly beneath his chin.

Yeah, he was dead.

Blood spatter covered his face, too, and it took Beck a moment to pick through what was left of the guy and figure out who this was.

"Hell," Beck mumbled.

He looked at the paper then. Hand-scrawled with just three sentences.

*I killed them. God forgive me. I can't live with what I've done.*

He left the note and body in place so the county CSI crew and the Rangers would have a pristine scene to process. That was if Nicole hadn't touched anything. He wanted them to find proof that this was indeed a suicide or if someone had staged it to look that way.

Everyone was waiting for Beck when he came back out, including Sgt. McKinney, the Ranger who was still investigating the tranquilizer gun incident from the night before. But it was Faith that Beck went to.

"It's not Darin," he told her.

Her breath broke, and she shattered. He felt the relief in her when he pulled her into his arms. "It's Nolan Wheeler."

Blinking back tears of relief, she looked up at him. "Nolan?" she repeated.

So did Pete and Nicole. "What was Nolan Wheeler doing here?" Pete asked.

"Apparently killing himself. There's a suicide note."

"I'll have a look," the Ranger insisted, going inside.

Faith shook her head. "Nolan committed suicide?"

Beck couldn't confirm that. "According to the note, he couldn't live with himself because of the murders he committed."

He saw the immediate doubt in Faith's eyes and knew what she was thinking. On the surface, Nolan wasn't the suicide type.

So did the man have some "help"?

"Why would he have done this?" Corey questioned.

Beck was short on answers. "Maybe he thought we were getting close to arresting him."

That was the only thing he could think of to justify

suicide. But why choose the Tanners' barn to do the deed? As far as Beck knew, Nolan wasn't familiar with the ranch.

"What were you doing in the barn?" he heard his brother ask Nicole.

Beck pushed aside his questions about Nolan because he was very interested in her answer.

Nicole, however, didn't seem pleased that all eyes were suddenly on her. "I was looking for my riding jacket. I thought I left it in there." Pete didn't jump to confirm her answer, so she sliced her gaze at Beck. "Why would I do anything to Nolan Wheeler? I hardly know him."

"You went to high school with him," Corey pointed out, earning him a nasty glare from both Pete and Nicole.

"I won't have Nicole accused of this or anything else," Pete snapped.

Nicole nodded crisply. "There's only one person here who had a reason to kill Nolan, and that's Faith."

Beck was about to defend her the way Pete had Nicole, but he spotted the Ranger walking back toward them. "I used my camera phone to take a picture of the suicide note and sent it straight to the crime lab. They'll compare it to Nolan's handwriting. We've got some samples on file that we've been comparing to the threats written in the attic."

"And did Nolan write those threats?" Faith wanted to know.

Sgt. McKinney shook his head. "The results are inconclusive, but we might have better luck with this suicide note since whoever wrote it didn't print."

Before the last word left the Ranger's mouth, Beck saw a movement out of the corner of his eye. He turned, automatically drawing his weapon. So did the Ranger and Corey. Pete shoved Nicole behind him.

Darin Matthews was walking straight toward them.

"Darin?" Faith called out.

Beck caught her arm to keep her from running toward her brother. Darin was limping and looked disheveled, maybe from the altercation he'd had with Roy.

"Don't shoot," Darin said. He lifted his hands in a show of surrender.

"Are you hurt?" Faith asked.

"Just my ankle. I think I sprained it when I was here earlier."

Roy took a step closer to the man. "You mean when I ran you off or when you killed Nolan?"

Darin froze, and his eyes widened. "Nolan's dead?" And he looked to Faith for confirmation.

"He's dead."

"I didn't do it. I came here because I've been sleeping in one of the barns while I've been in town looking for evidence to clear my name. I didn't kill anyone, and I didn't help Nolan do it, either." He took in a weary breath. "But I'm tired now. I need to rest."

"You'll have to get your rest at the sheriff's office," Beck let him know. He walked closer and patted Darin down. He wasn't armed, but in addition to the limp, there was a nasty gash on the back on his head. It was no longer bleeding, but it looked as if it could use some stitches.

The Ranger's cell phone rang, and he stepped aside to take the call.

"Darin will have to be cuffed," Beck let Faith know, and he kept a grip on her until after Corey had done that.

When he let go of her, Faith ran to Darin and hugged him. "I want to go with him."

Beck didn't even try to argue with her. He knew it would do no good. He motioned for Corey to get Darin into the cruiser. He and Faith would follow it, first to the emergency room and then to his office, where he'd eventually have to lock up Darin.

"I'll do whatever you need me to do," Darin insisted. He looked at Faith. "You're not in danger anymore. Nolan can't hurt you."

"And I'll help you," Faith promised. "I have attorney friends who can defend you if you're charged with anything. There's a lot of evidence, and when it's all examined and processed, I think it'll prove you're innocent."

Beck hoped the same thing.

Nicole walked closer to them. "Now that this is over, and the killer's been caught, there's no reason for Faith to stay at your house any longer. We can finally get back to the way things were."

Beck shook his head. "This case isn't settled." And Faith would stay with him until it was.

He didn't want to think beyond that.

"We might be one step closer to getting things settled," the Ranger announced, rejoining them. "That was the crime lab. We'll need to do more analysis, of course, but the handwriting expert says the suicide note appears to be a match to Nolan Wheeler's."

"So he did write that note," Nicole concluded.

Beck considered a different theory. "Perhaps he wrote it under duress?" While a gun was pointed to his head?

The Ranger shrugged. "Maybe, but according to

the expert, there are no obvious indications of hesitation. There probably would have been if he'd been forced to write it."

Well, that put a new light on things. Nolan had confessed to the murders in that note. Maybe Darin had been telling the truth about his lack of involvement? Maybe he wasn't a killer, and Nolan had been the one to orchestrate all of this so he could get the money from Sherry's blackmail scheme and her estate.

"We should go." Beck caught Faith's arm and led her toward his cruiser.

With her barely out of the hospital, he didn't like the idea of her having to accompany him to the station, but he didn't want her alone, either. Besides, she would want to be there when Beck questioned Darin. And when the questioning was done, the loose ends would be tied up into a neat little package.

So why did Beck have this uneasy feeling in the pit of his stomach?

Why did he feel that Faith was in even more danger than ever?

# *Chapter Thirteen*

Faith's mind was racing. She was mentally exhausted after spending most of the afternoon with her brother. But she was also hopeful.

Because soon she'd get to see her little girl.

She'd already called Marita, and the nanny had told her they would be on their way back when they got everything packed up. With luck, Aubrey would be home within the next three hours.

Well, not home exactly. But back at Beck's house, where they'd stay another day or two until she could decide something more permanent.

She climbed out of the cruiser, went inside the house and into the kitchen. Because it suddenly seemed to take too much energy to go any farther, she leaned against the wall and tried to absorb everything.

So much had happened in the past twenty hours. Too much to grasp at once.

Nolan was dead and no longer a threat to Aubrey and her. Her brother was at the LaMesa Springs hospital receiving treatment for the head wound he'd gotten from the altercation with Roy. Once the doctor released him,

Darin would still have to undergo an intense interrogation. Maybe the evidence against him would even have to go to a grand jury. But Beck had promised her that Darin would be given fair treatment and that he personally was going to recommend that any assessment come from the county mental health officials.

Her brother might finally get the help he needed.

Beck came in behind her, took off his jacket and hung it on the hook on the mudroom door. "How's your neck?" he asked.

It took her a moment to realize what he meant. The tranquilizer dart wound. Even though it hadn't been that long since the injury, she'd forgotten all about it. "It's fine," she assured him.

The corner of his mouth lifted. A weary smile. "You're not feeling any pain because Aubrey will be here soon."

Faith couldn't argue with that, so she returned the smile. She took off her coat and hung it next to his. "Thank you for letting us stay with you."

It seemed as if he changed his mind a dozen times about what to say. "You're welcome."

His response was sincere, she didn't doubt that, but there was something else. Something simmering beneath the surface. "Your family won't like me being here. I'll make plans to leave tomorrow."

No smile this time. He took off his shoulder holster, and with the weapon inside, he placed it on top of the fridge. "No hurry. I don't want you to make any decisions based on my family. Truth is, I'm fed up with them. And I'd like for Aubrey, Marita and you to stay here for as long as you like. Or until at least we have everything sorted out with your brother. It's a big place, lots of room, and we can get to know each other better."

"You've known me for years," she pointed out.

He lowered his head. Touched his lips to hers. "But I want to know you *better.*"

The kiss was over before it even started. It was hardly more than a peck. But it slid through her from her lips all the way to her toes.

"That sounds sexual." Or maybe that was wishful thinking on her part.

"It is," he drawled. "But the invitation isn't good for tonight. Tonight, you'll rest, take a hot bath and spend time with Aubrey when she gets here. In a day or two, I'll work on getting you into my bed again."

There it was. More heat. She'd been attracted to men before but never like this. Nothing had ever felt like this. It scared her, but at the same time, she wanted more.

"Don't look at me like that," he warned.

She touched the front of his shirt with her fingertips. "Like what?"

"Like you want to get naked with me."

"Oh." Maybe she looked that way because that's exactly what she wanted. "I'm at a disadvantage here. I've spent my entire adult life pulling back from men. I don't know how to stop you from treating me like glass. I don't know how to make you take me the way you would a woman with lots of experience. I don't know how to seduce you."

He shrugged. "Breathe."

Faith blinked. "Excuse me?"

He leaned in, whispered in her ear, "This is all about

you, Faith. Just you. To seduce me, all you have to do is breathe and say yes."

"Yes." She pulled in a loud breath, and with that, his mouth came to hers.

This time, it wasn't a peck, it was a full-fledged kiss. His mouth moved over hers as if he knew exactly what to do to set her on fire.

It worked.

Faith leaned against him—until she could no longer do the thing that had set all of this into motion. She couldn't breathe. And she didn't care. She'd take Beck's kisses over breathing any day.

His left arm went around her waist, and he pulled her to him. The embrace was gentle. Unlike the kiss that had turned French and a little rough.

Faith broke the intimate contact so he could see her face. "No treating me like glass," she reminded him. "And I'd rather not rest tonight if you don't mind."

He stared at her, and she could see the debate that stirred the muscles in his jaw. "All right."

That was the only warning she got before he hoisted her up. Face-to-face. Body against body. And he delivered some of those kisses to the front of her neck and then into the V of her top.

Faith automatically wrapped her arms and legs around him. His sex touched hers and sent a shiver of heat dancing through her. She wanted him naked, now.

She went after his shirt as he carried her toward his bedroom. Buttons popped and flew, pinging on the floor, and her frenzy of need for him only fueled the fire. She got his shirt off and kissed his neck. Then his chest.

He made a throaty sound of approval and, off

balance, he rammed his shoulder into the doorjamb. Faith wanted to ask if he was okay, but he obviously was.

Beck kissed her even harder, and instead of taking her to the bed, he stopped just short of it, and with her pressed between him and the mattress, he slid them to the floor. While he kissed her blind, he unzipped her jeans and peeled them off her. Bra and panties, too, leaving her naked. He quickly covered her left nipple with his mouth.

The sensation shot through her.

His hand went lower, between her legs, and his fingers found her. He slipped his index finger through the slippery moisture of her body and touched her so intimately that Faith could have sworn she saw stars.

"Breathe," he reminded her.

She thought she might be breathing, but couldn't tell. The only thing she knew for sure was that she wanted him to continue with those slippery, clever strokes.

And he did.

He touched and created a delicious friction that brought her just to the edge.

Faith caught her breath and caught onto his hand. "You, inside me," she managed to say, though she didn't know how she'd gotten out the words. Speech suddenly seemed very complex and not entirely necessary.

She shoved down his zipper, which took some doing. He was huge and hard, making it difficult for her to free him from his jeans and boxers.

Even though her need was burning her to ash, she took a moment to fulfill a fantasy she'd had for years.

She got him out of those jeans, took Beck in her hand and slid her fingers down the length of him, all the while guiding him right to where she wanted him to go.

He reacted with a male sound deep within his chest. He buried his face in her hair. His breath, hot against his skin. His mouth, tense now, muffled a groan, and he kissed her. His tongue parted the seam of her lips as his hard sex touched the softness of hers.

Her vision blurred. She reached to pull him closer. Deeper into her. But he stopped and cursed.

"Condom," he gutted out.

Still cursing, he reached over, rummaged through his nightstand drawer and produced a condom. He hurried, but it still seemed an eternity. The moment he had it on, Faith pulled him back to her.

Despite the urgency that she could feel in every part of him, Beck entered her slowly. Gently. Inch by inch. While he watched her. That wasn't difficult to do since they were face-to-face with her straddling him. He was watching to see if he was hurting her.

He wasn't.

The only pain she felt was from the hard ache of unfilled need. A need that Beck was more than capable of satisfying.

She could see how much this gentleness was costing him. Beck didn't want to hold back anything, and Faith made sure he didn't. She thrust her hips forward.

Beck cursed again.

"It's better than I thought it'd be," she mumbled. A shock since she'd been positive it would be pretty darn good.

"Yeah," he said.

He stilled a moment to let her adjust to this intimate invasion, but the stillness only lasted a few seconds and a kiss. He moved, sliding into her. Drawing back. Then sliding in even deeper. Each motion took her higher. Closer. Until her focus honed in on the one thing she had to have.

Release.

Beck had taken her to this hot, crazy place. He'd made her feel things she'd only imagined. And he just kept making her feel.

He slid his hand between their bodies, and with him sliding in and out of her, he touched her with his fingers, matching the frenetic stokes of his sex. He kept touching. Kept moving. The need got stronger. Until she was sure she couldn't bear the heat any longer.

Beck seemed to understand that. He kissed her. Touched her. Went deep inside her. A triple assault. And it happened. In a flash. Her orgasm wracked through her, filling her and giving her primal release.

*Breathe,* Faith reminded herself. *Breathe.*

There were no barriers. No bad blood. Nothing to stop her from realizing the truth.

She was in love with Beckett Tanner.

WELL, FAITH WAS BREATHING all right.

Her chest was pumping as if starved for air, and each pump pushed her sweat-dampened breasts against his chest. There was a look of total amazement on her face.

She was practically glowing.

Beck knew he was somewhat responsible for giving her that look, and when his brain caught up with the now sated part of his body, he might try to figure out what he was going to do about that look. And about what'd just happened.

For now though, he just held her and tried not to make any annoying male grunts when the aftershocks of her climax reminded him that he was still inside her. Not that he needed such a reminder.

"That was worth waiting for," she mumbled.

He kissed her, tried to think of something clever to say and settled for another kiss. But he would have to address this sooner or later. Faith obviously wasn't a casual sex kind of person. Neither was he. But it suddenly felt as if he had more than a normal responsibility here. A commitment, maybe.

After all, he was her *first*.

He certainly hadn't expected to have that title once he was past the age of twenty. Maybe she'd have some emotional fallout from this.

Maybe even some regrets.

Beck realized she was staring at him. Her breathing had settled. There were no more aftershocks. But she had her head tilted to the side, and she was studying him.

"What?" he prompted.

"I'm just trying to get inside your head." She smiled. It was tentative. Perhaps even a facade. "Don't worry. This doesn't mean we're going steady or anything." Still smiling, she moved off him and stood.

Beck caught onto her hand before she could move too far from him. All in all, it wasn't a bad vantage point. He was still sitting. Looking up at her. She was naked. Beautiful. Glistening with perspiration. And his scent was on her.

He wanted her all over again.

"I need a drink of water," she let him know. She leaned down and kissed him. "Then I think I'll take a bath before Aubrey gets here."

He had some cleaning up to do, too, and rather than sit there and watch her dress, Beck got up, gathered his clothes from the floor and went into the adjoining bathroom.

While he cleaned up and put his jeans back on, he glanced at the tub. Should he run her a bath? Probably not. It would only lead to more sex. Once was enough for her tonight. Plus, despite her "going steady" remark, she had some feelings she needed to work through.

He certainly did.

The house phone rang, and he went back into the bedroom to answer it. "Sheriff Tanner."

"It's Corey. Is Darin Matthews with you?" His words were harried and borderline frantic.

That put a knot in Beck's stomach. "No. He's supposed to be at the hospital with you."

Corey cursed. "Darin was sedated so I went to the vending machine to get a Coke. When I got back, he wasn't in his bed. I guess he wasn't sedated as much as I thought. I've looked all through the building and the parking lot. He's not here."

Darin couldn't have gotten far with that injured leg. Beck hoped. Unless he stole a car.

"Don't put out an APB just yet, but if one of the Rangers is still around, let him know so he can look for him. Faith and I will drive around, too, and see if we can spot him. Darin's probably looking for her anyway."

"One more thing," Corey said before Beck could end

the call. "The Ranger lab in Austin put a rush on that DNA test you ordered. They faxed the results over, and the dispatcher brought it to me while I was looking for Darin."

Great. He needed those results, but he had to resolve this problem with Darin first. "The results will keep," Beck let him know.

Cursing under his breath, Beck hung up and reached for his boots. He should probably call Marita and Tracy and delay Aubrey's homecoming, just in case Darin had some kind of psychotic episode.

Beck reached for the phone again, but stopped when he heard the soft sound. A thud. He stilled and listened. But there wasn't another sound. Just the uneasy feeling that all was not right.

"Faith?" he called out.

Nothing.

That knot in his stomach tightened. Hell. Why hadn't she answered?

The answer that came to mind had him grabbing the gun from the nightstand.

Beck started for the kitchen.

## Chapter Fourteen

Faith opened the cupboard and reached for a glass. But reaching for it was as far as she got.

The lights went out.

She heard footsteps behind her. Before she could pick through the darkness to see who was behind her, an arm went around her neck, putting her in a choke hold.

A hand clamped over her mouth, and she felt the cold steel of a gun barrel shoved against her right temple.

Oh, God. What was happening?

Nolan was dead. The danger was over. Who was this person, and what was going on?

She didn't wait for the answers. Faith rammed her elbow into her attacker's belly. She might as well have rammed it into a brick wall because other than a soft grunt, the person didn't react.

"What do you want?" she tried to say, but his hand muffled any sound.

Still, there were sounds. Footsteps, both his and hers, as he started to drag her in the direction of the back door. Beck would likely hear the sounds, even though he might still be on the phone dealing with the call that'd come in.

Once that call was finished, he would begin to wonder what was taking her so long to get a drink of water.

Then Beck would come looking for her.

And this person might shoot him.

He jammed the gun even harder against her temple when she started to struggle, and Faith had to try to come to terms with the fact that she might be murdered tonight. She thought of Aubrey, of her precious little girl. And of Beck. He would blame himself for this because he hadn't been there to protect her. But Faith didn't want him there. She wanted to live, but not at the expense of Beck being killed.

The man opened the back door, and cold air rushed inside, cutting what little breath she had. He tried to push her outside, but Faith dug in her heels. If he got her out of the house and away from Beck, he'd just take her to a secondary crime scene where he'd do God knows what to her.

But why?

And that brought her back to the question of whom.

Had Nolan hired someone to do this last deed? A way of reaching out from beyond the grave to settle an old score with her?

Of course, there was another possibility. One she didn't want to consider—maybe somehow her brother had gotten free. Maybe he really was a killer after all and had come to eliminate the last member of their family.

"Faith?" she heard Beck call out.

Her attacker froze for just a moment and then resumed the struggle to get her out the door. She tried to warn Beck, but her assailant's hand prevented that.

"What the hell's going on?" Beck called.

Though it was pitch-dark, she spotted him in the hallway opening just off the kitchen. She also saw him lift his gun and take aim.

The attacker stopped trying to shove her out the door, and he pivoted, placing her in front of him. He even crouched slightly down so that his head was partially behind hers.

She was now a human shield.

"Who are you?" Beck demanded. He squinted, obviously trying to adjust to the darkness. He reached out for the light switch on the wall next to him.

"Don't," her attacker growled. He kept his voice throaty and low, but there were no doubts that this was a man. A strong one. He had her in a death grip, and the barrel of the gun cut into her skin.

Beck didn't turn on the light, but he kept his gun aimed.

"I'm leaving with her," the man said. He was obviously trying to disguise his voice. That meant Beck and she probably knew him.

Inching sideways and with her still in front of him to block Beck's shot, the man started dragging her back to the door.

Faith didn't know whether to fight or not. If she did resist, he might just shoot Beck. However, the same might happen if she cooperated.

Beck inched closer as well, and because she was watching him, she saw his eyes widen. He didn't drop his gun, but he did lower it.

"Pete?" Beck called out.

The man's muscles went stiff, and he stopped. She heard every word of his harshly whispered profanity.

"What the hell do you think you're doing?" Beck demanded. He came even closer.

"Stop," the man said. Not a muffled whisper this time. She clearly heard his voice.

It was indeed Pete, Beck's brother.

"Well?" Beck prompted. "What the hell are you doing?"

"What's necessary." With that, Pete jammed the gun even harder against her. She could smell the liquor on his breath, but he wasn't drunk. He was too steady for that.

"What's necessary?" Beck spat out. "How did you even get in here?"

"You gave Dad the codes to disarm the security system and I used the key you gave me for emergencies. I didn't want you to be part of this," Pete said to Beck. "I wanted to take care of her before you noticed she was missing. She's a loose end."

Beck shook his head, and his expression said it all. He couldn't believe this was happening. "Put down your gun."

"I can't. I have to fix this." Pete groaned and took his hand from her mouth. "I've made a mess of my life."

"You can fix things the legal way," Beck insisted. His voice was calm, and he took another step toward them. "Put down the gun."

"It's too late for that. I killed them, Beck. I killed them all."

Oh, God. It was true. Pete was a killer, and he had her in his grips.

"You mean you killed Sherry and Annie?" Beck clarified.

"Yeah, I did. But it was all Sherry's fault. I swear she

tricked me into that affair. When I saw her at the Moonlight Bar, she came onto me, got me drunk and then took pictures of me when I was sleeping. She blackmailed me. And I gave her the money. I gave her exactly what she wanted—ten thousand dollars that I got from Dad's accounts. Look where it got me."

"Start from the beginning. What happened?" Beck asked.

"The beginning? I'm not sure when it all started. But killing Sherry was an accident. I swear. I used the tranquilizer gun from the stables and drugged her so I could reason with her. But the drug wore off too soon, and when she started struggling, I had to strangle her."

"It wasn't premeditated," Beck explained. "You could maybe plea down to manslaughter. That's why you need to put down the gun so we can talk."

"Talking's not going to save me. Sherry's death might not have been premeditated, but the others were."

Until that statement, Beck had managed to maintain some of his cop's persona, but the grim reality of Pete's confession etched his face with not just concern but shock. "What do you mean?"

"After I killed Sherry, I tried to get the money back so Dad and Nicole wouldn't find out, but Annie wouldn't give it to me. She said she wanted it and more. A lot more. She wanted fifty thousand dollars. That's when I had to kill her. I couldn't keep paying her off, and I knew she'd tell Nicole."

It was so hard for Faith to hear all of this. She hadn't been close to Sherry or her mother, but both of them had been killed for money. For greed. And to cover up an affair that Sherry had probably orchestrated just so she could blackmail Pete. If he hadn't been thinking from below the belt, Pete might have figured it out before things got this far.

"I thought after I killed Annie that it'd be over," Pete continued, his voice weary and dry. "But I got another letter demanding more money. I thought it came from Nolan. That's why I put a gun to his head and made him write that suicide note. But he insisted right up to the end that he hadn't sent any blackmail letters."

"You killed him anyway," Beck said. It wasn't a question.

"Nolan Wheeler deserved to die." Pete's voice was suddenly defiant. "He'd been skirting the law for years. I did the world a favor."

"The world might not agree," Beck countered. "I certainly don't. You killed three people, and you're holding a gun on your brother and the assistant district attorney. Where's the justice in that?"

Pete stayed quiet a moment. "It'll be my own form of justice. I can't let either of you live. Especially Faith. This afternoon there was another blackmail letter in the mailbox. She put it there. I know she did. There couldn't be anyone else."

"You don't know that. It could be one of Sherry's friends. Besides, Faith's been with me all day. She couldn't have put the letter in the mailbox."

"I don't believe you," Pete practically shouted. "You're covering for her because you're sleeping with her. You chose her over your own family."

"Maybe I did," Beck conceded. Unlike Pete, he kept his voice level and calm though Faith didn't know how he managed to do that. "But it's my job to protect her." He took another step toward them. "Put the gun down, Pete, and let's talk this out."

"No. No more talking. I'd wanted to do this clean and nearly succeeded last night. I got the tranquilizer in her, but then you came to the rescue. Just like tonight. But the difference is, tonight I'll kill you, too."

"I'm your brother," Beck reminded him. "Think what killing me would do the family."

"I can't think about that. I have to protect Nicole. She's my first and only concern. I have to make sure she never learns about any of this. The only way for that to happen is for you to die."

Pete re-aimed his gun.

At Beck.

Faith felt the muscles in Pete's arm tense. She saw the realization of what was about to happen on Beck's face. He couldn't shoot at his brother because he might hit her. Pete, however, had no concern about that since he intended to kill them both anyway.

She yelled for Beck to get down. With the sound of her voice echoing through the house, Faith turned, ramming her shoulder into Pete. He hardly budged from the impact, but it was enough to shake his aim.

The bullet that Pete fired slammed into the wall next to the fridge.

Beck lunged at them, and the hard tackle sent all three of them to the floor. Beck's own gun went flying, and it skittered across the floor. And the race was on to see which one would come up with Pete's gun.

Faith managed to untangle herself from the mix. She got to her feet and slapped on the light. Pete and Beck were practically the same size, and they were in a life-and-death struggle.

She waited until she spotted Pete's hand. And the gun. Faith went for it, dropping back to the floor, and she latched on to his wrist. Somehow, she had to keep that gun pointed away from Beck.

Beck drew back his fist and slammed it into Pete's face. The man was either tough as nails or the adrenaline had made him immune to the pain because he hardly reacted. In fact, Pete twisted his body and slammed his forearm into her jaw. The impact nearly knocked the breath from her, but somehow Faith managed to hang on to his wrist. She dug in her nails and clawed at any part of his flesh that she could reach.

Beck threw another punch. And another. The third one was the charm. Pete's head flopped back onto the tile floor. Dazed and bleeding from his mouth and nose, he groaned and mumbled something indistinguishable.

"The gun," Beck said.

Beck wrenched it from his brother's hand. He pulled in a hard breath and reached again, this time to roll Pete on his stomach so he could subdue him.

"Call nine-one-one," Beck told her.

"You're sure?" she asked, though she knew he had no choice. This was attempted murder. But Pete was still his brother. A lesser man would have wanted to try to resolve this without the law and tried to keep it a family secret.

Beck nodded. "I'm sure. Make the call."

She got up to do that, but before Faith even made it to her feet, the back door flew open, hitting her squarely in the back and sending her plummeting into Beck.

"Oh, my God," someone said.

Nicole.

Pete used the distraction of his wife's arrival to ram his elbow into Beck, and grab his gun.

Faith couldn't scramble away from him in time. Pete latched on to her hair and dragged her in front of him again.

"January fourteenth," Pete said as if in triumph. "Faith dies."

HIS BROTHER'S WORDS WERE like stabs from a switch-blade. It was the threat written in the attic. A threat Beck hadn't announced to anyone other than law enforcement, which meant Pete had been the one to paint that threat on Faith's attic walls.

Oh, man. Things had really gone crazy. And worse, it might turn deadly if he didn't do something now to stop all of this.

Beck's gaze connected with Faith's. She was scared. And shocked. But he could also see determination. She wasn't just going to stand there and let Pete kill them. She was a fighter, but this fight might cause Pete to pull that trigger even faster.

"Pete, what's going on?" Nicole asked.

Nicole looked at Beck, her eyes searching for a logical answer. But he couldn't give her one. There was no logic in any of this. Another of Pete's affairs had gotten him into trouble, and he'd been willing to kill to keep his secret.

"Pete killed Annie and Sherry Matthews. Nolan Wheeler, too," Beck explained to Nicole. "Now, he's going to put his gun down so we can deal with this."

Beck hoped.

"I killed them for you, Nicole," Pete insisted.

She gasped and stepped back. Good. So Nicole wasn't in on this. Maybe, just maybe, she could talk Pete into surrendering.

"Tell Pete to put his gun down," Beck instructed Nicole.

She gave a choppy nod. "Please, Pete. Do as Beck says."

"Faith's blackmailing me. She sent me a letter today. Left it in the mailbox—"

"No. She didn't." Nicole shook her head. "I sent the last two letters."

Beck hadn't thought there could be any more surprises tonight, but he'd obviously been wrong. "You?" he questioned. "Why?"

Tears filled Nicole's eyes. "Sherry called me two months ago and told me about her affair with Pete. She faxed me copies of the pictures of them together."

"Oh, God." Pete groaned. "I'm sorry. So sorry."

"I know." Nicole blinked back the tears, and her voice was eerily calm. "But I was upset, and I wanted to leave you—after I punished you. So, after Sherry and Annie were killed, I sent a third letter. This afternoon, I put the fourth one in the mailbox. I wanted you to suffer. I wanted you to think that your indiscretion would be punished for a long, long time."

Pete cursed. He glanced at Faith and then cursed some more.

"Faith didn't do anything wrong," Beck said. "You need to let her go."

"Yes," Nicole agreed. "Let her go. Let Beck handle this."

"I can't. Don't you see what has to happen here? I've already put the plan in place. I waited at the hospital until I could get Darin alone, and I forced him to leave with me. There are no security cameras in the entire place so it was easy. Then I left him on the side of the road about a mile from here."

"No," Faith mumbled.

Beck silently mumbled the same. With Darin hurt and possibility medicated, he shouldn't be out on his own on a cold winter night. It was a cliché, but he could literally die in a ditch somewhere.

"Darin will try to go home, but he won't have an alibi," Pete continued. "He'll be blamed for Beck's and Faith's murders. Then we can start over, Nicole. I swear, no more affairs."

That just pissed Beck off. His brother was willing to kill Faith and him rather than take responsibility for what he'd done. Somehow, he had to get Faith out of harm's way and subdue Pete.

"Do you hear yourself?" Beck snapped. "I knew you were self-centered and egotistical, but I had no idea you'd stoop to this. Think it through. You plan to kill me and Faith in front of Nicole? What kind of future can you have with that hanging over your heads?"

"Beck's right," Nicole added. "I could never stay with you after what you've done."

"You tricked me with those letters!" Pete shouted.

*"Letters?"* Nicole threw right back at him. "I didn't murder anyone. Nor would I. Did you honestly think I could live with a killer?"

Pete slowly aimed his attention at Nicole. The change in his brother's expression wasn't subtle. Rage sliced through his eyes, and the muscles corded on his face. "I did this all for you, and this is how you treat me?"

"You didn't do this for Nicole." Beck wanted to get Pete's attention off Nicole and Faith and back onto him. Because it looked as if his brother was about to start shooting at any minute. "You did this to cover up what you'd done. Well, the covering up has to stop."

"Who says?" He pushed Faith onto her knees and put the gun to the back of her head.

She looked up. Her eyes met Beck's. "I love you," she said, silently mouthing the words.

Oh, man. Oh. Man. That hit him, hard, but he knew he couldn't think about it. Later—and there would be a later—he'd deal with her confession.

A sound shot through the room.

Beck was certain he lost ten years of his life. It took him a moment to realize that Pete hadn't fired. The phone was ringing.

"Don't answer that," Pete ordered. "You," he said to Nicole. "Get down on the floor next to her."

Nicole frantically shook her head. "You're going to shoot me?"

"Yeah." This was no longer the voice of his brother. It was the voice of a cold, calculated killer. "I love you, Nicole. I always will. But I won't give up my life for you. I'm not going to jail for you."

The answering machine kicked in on the fifth ring. "Faith, it's Marita. Pick up."

"No," Faith whispered. She repeated it as Marita's cheerful voice poured through the room.

"I guess you're celebrating, but I wanted you to know we'll be there in about ten minutes. Aubrey's sacked out, but I'll wake her when we arrive so you can get some hugs and kisses."

Hell. Ten minutes. He couldn't have Marita, Tracy and especially Aubrey walking into this.

"I gave Marita an emergency key," Beck let Faith know. And that meant if they didn't answer the door, which they wouldn't be able to do at this point, then Marita might let herself in.

"You couldn't hurt a child," Beck told Pete, trying one last time to reason with him.

Pete met him eye-to-eye. "I'm fighting for my life. I can and will hurt anyone who gets in my way."

Beck believed him. This wouldn't end with a successful surrender. It would end only when he managed to stop Pete. He might even have to kill his own brother. But he would if it came down to that.

He wouldn't allow Pete to hurt anyone else.

"Go ahead," Beck instructed Nicole. "Get on the floor."

The tears were spilling down her cheeks now, and her eyes were wide with terror.

"Trust me," Beck added. "Get on the floor."

Nicole gave a shaky nod. Using her right hand to steady herself, she started to lower herself to her knees.

Beck waited.

Watching Pete.

His brother glanced at Nicole. Just as Beck had figured he would do. It was just a glance. But in that glance, Pete took his attention off Beck and Faith.

That was the break Beck had been waiting for.

He dove at Pete.

Though Beck was moving as fast as he could, everything seemed to slow to a crawl. He saw the split-second realization in Pete's eyes. And then Pete reacted. He didn't turn the gun on Beck.

But on Faith.

Pete lowered the barrel of the semiautomatic right toward the back of Faith's head.

And he fired.

## Chapter Fifteen

Faith moved as quickly as she could, but she figured it wasn't nearly fast enough. She braced herself.

Death would come before she even knew if Beck had heard her. "I love you," she'd said. It might be the last time she ever had a chance to say that to anyone.

She was feeling and hearing way too much for Pete's bullet to have killed her. Instead, she realized that it'd smacked into the tile floor less than two feet from her.

Pete's bullet had missed her.

The sound of the fired shot was deafening, and it roared through her head, stabbing into her eardrums. It was excruciating, but since she could feel it, she knew she was very much alive.

So was Beck, thank God.

With his momentum at full speed, Beck crashed into Pete, and into her. Pete's gun dislodged from his hand and landed somewhere behind them.

"No!" Nicole yelled. She scrambled to the side to get away from the collision.

However, because Faith was directly in front of Pete, she wasn't so lucky. She was caught in the impact, again. Caught in the middle of the struggle. But this time, the stakes were even higher.

Aubrey was on her way there.

"Run!" Beck told her.

From the corner of her eye, she saw Nicole do just that. She threw open the back door and rushed out into the night. Maybe the woman would call the deputy. But as distraught as Nicole was, Faith couldn't rely on her for help. She and Beck had to stop Pete.

"Now!" Beck snarled to her. "Get out of here."

Faith wiggled her way out of the fight and somehow managed to get to her feet. But before she could run, Pete latched on to her ankle and tried to pull her back down. She fought, kicking at him, but he was pumped on adrenaline now and was fighting like a crazy man with triple his normal strength.

Then things got worse. The doorbell rang.

"We're here," Marita called out.

Marita's announcement nearly caused Faith to panic, but she forced herself to concentrate on the task. She gave Pete another hard kick, and that broke the vising grip he had on her. She felt him reach for her, and he groped at the floor.

Faith ran. But not out the back as Nicole had done.

Frantically, she looked around for Beck's gun. She didn't see it, and it took her a moment to figure out why.

Pete had it.

Oh, God.

Pete had the gun.

"Come in!" Pete shouted to Marita, dodging a fist that Beck had tried to send his way. "Beck needs help."

"No," Faith countered. "Stay back." And she hoped they'd heard her and would do as she said.

She looked around the floor for another weapon and remembered Beck's service pistol. Faith grabbed it from the top of the fridge where he'd put it right after they'd returned from seeing Darin.

"Stop!" she yelled.

Pete didn't. Neither did Beck. Pete managed to land a hard punch on Beck's jaw, and the momentum sent him backward. The two men weren't separated for long because Beck dove at him.

The doorbell rang again, and it was followed by a knock. "What's going on in there?" Tracy asked.

Faith hurried to him and held out his service revolver. Beck snatched it from her hand and got up off the floor.

Pete did the same.

And the two brothers met gun-to-gun.

"Don't," Beck warned, his voice a threatening growl.

The corner of Pete's mouth lifted. A twisted, sick smile. "You think a bullet can go through your front door?" He didn't wait for Beck to answer. "Because I do. God knows what a bullet would hit…"

Pete didn't have to aim in that direction. Faith realized his gun was already pointed there. Just to Beck's right. And that put it in line with the door.

Oh, God. That nearly brought Faith to her knees. Her baby was in danger.

"Try to warn them and I'll shoot through the door," Pete warned. "I have nothing to lose."

Faith didn't cower. "And you have nothing to gain from hurting my child."

"True. But it'll be nice to see you suffer."

Every inch of Beck was primed for the fight, and his face was dotted with sweat from the struggle. "Faith did nothing to you."

"Yes, she did. She came back. She made me think she'd written that blackmail letter. She made me believe I had to stop her. The woman's just bad luck, Beck. She always has been."

Faith saw Beck's finger tense on the trigger, and he had his attention fastened to his brother's own trigger finger. One move, and Beck would shoot him. Faith didn't doubt that. But what she did fear was that even if Beck shot him that Pete would still manage to shoot.

Aubrey could still be in danger.

She heard the scrape of metal, a key being inserted into a lock, and she glanced at the front door.

Just as it opened.

"No!" Faith shouted. And she automatically turned in the direction of the door. She had to block any shot that Pete might take.

She only made it one step before the bullet rang out.

BECK DIDN'T EVEN WAIT to see where Pete's bullet had hit.

Or who.

He couldn't think about that. Right now, he had to stop Pete from firing again. Each shot could be lethal.

Still, Beck couldn't stop the rage that roared through him. Pete had put Aubrey and Faith in danger. To save his own butt, his brother had been willing to hurt a child.

Beck grabbed Pete's right arm. He wanted to shoot his brother. To end this here and now. But Beck couldn't risk another shot being fired.

Not with Aubrey and Faith so close.

Faith yelled something, but the blood crashing in Beck's ears made it impossible to hear. Besides, Beck only wanted to concentrate on the fight.

Beck dropped his gun so he could use both hands to try to gain control of Pete. His brother was fighting him, trying to re-aim his gun in the direction of the door. Beck wasn't able to get his finger off the trigger.

Pete fired again. The shot landed somewhere in the ceiling, and white powdery plaster began to rain down on them. Good. As long as that shot wasn't near the others.

Beck heard the sound then. A cry.

*Aubrey.*

Every muscle in his body turned to iron. *God, was the child hurt?* Or maybe it was Faith who'd taken the bullet. Maybe both were injured. Hell. He could lose them and all because of his selfish SOB of a brother.

"You can't save them," Pete growled.

It was exactly what Beck needed to hear. Not that he needed a reminder of what was at stake, but his brother's threat was the jolt that gave Beck that extra boost of adrenaline. Nothing was going to stop him from saving Aubrey and Faith.

*Nothing.*

From the corner of his eye, Beck saw Faith running toward the front door. There was no color in her face, and she appeared to be trembling. But she was headed in Aubrey's direction. Hopefully, she'd take the child and run. He wanted them as far away from there as possible.

With both his hands clamped onto Pete's right arm and wrist, Beck used his body and strength to maneuver Pete backward. Toward the wall. Pete didn't go willingly. He cursed, kicked and spat at Beck, all the while using his left fist to pound any part of Beck that he could reach.

Beck slammed him against the wall. The impact was so hard that it rattled the nearby kitchen cabinets. Still, Pete didn't stop struggling. Beck didn't stop, either. He bashed Pete's right hand against the granite countertop. The first time he didn't dislodge the gun.

But the second time he did. Pete's gun fell onto the granite.

Even though he was unarmed, Pete was still dangerous. So Beck didn't waste even a second of time. He caught onto his brother's shoulder and whirled him around, jamming his face and chest against the wall between the cabinets and the mudroom door. There wasn't much room to maneuver, but Beck wanted to get Pete onto the floor, facedown, so he could better subdue him.

Pete didn't cooperate with that, either, but Beck had the upper hand. With his forearm against the nape of Pete's neck, he put pressure on the backs of his brother's knees until he could get him belly down onto the tile floor.

By the time it was done, both Pete and he were fighting for air. Both of them were covered in sweat and blood from their cuts and scrapes.

But it was finally close to being over.

"Faith, are you all right?" Beck called out.

Since he'd expended most of his breath in the fight, he had to repeat it before it had any sound. And then he waited.

Praying.

He didn't hear her say anything. No reassurance that she was okay. But he could hear footsteps. Frantic ones.

Something was going on in the living room. Before he could call out to Faith again, there was another sound.

The back door opened.

It was Nicole.

"Let Pete go," she said. Her voice was trembling as much as her hand.

And she had a gun in her hand.

Beck cursed. He didn't need another battle when he hadn't even finished the first one.

"Nicole," Pete said through his gusting breath. "I knew you'd come back for me."

"I didn't do this for you. What you did was stupid, Pete, but I can't let you go to jail. Despite what you've done, you're still my husband. Part of me still loves you." She turned her teary eyes to Beck and pointed the gun right at him. "I'm a good shot," she reminded him. "Now let him go."

"Go where? Pete's a killer. What if he turns his anger on you?"

"He won't. I'm the reason he killed."

"He could hurt someone else," Beck reminded her. "You'd be responsible for that."

"What do I care if Faith Matthews and her bastard child are hurt?" Her attention went back to Pete. "I'll get you out of this, and then we'll be even. I want you to leave and never come back."

That wouldn't be good enough. Beck knew Pete wouldn't stay away. As long as his brother was alive and free, Faith and Aubrey would be in danger.

"I can't let him go," Beck insisted.

"Then I'll have to shoot you," Nicole insisted right back.

And she would.

Beck could see it in her eyes.

She'd already crossed over and left reason behind. She was going to save Pete whether he deserved it or not.

Nicole adjusted her aim so that it was right at Beck's shoulder. She wasn't going for the kill, but it didn't matter. The shot could still be deadly, and even if it only incapacitated him, it would leave the others vulnerable.

Cursing under his breath, Beck readied himself to take evasive action. He'd roll to the right, dropping to Pete's side. It might cause Nicole to think twice about shooting. But then it would give Pete the opportunity to break free.

"Nicole!" someone yelled.

*Faith.*

*Hell. She'd come back.*

Nicole automatically looked in the direction of Faith's voice. Beck couldn't see her. She was behind him.

But he saw the movement of something flying through the air.

Nicole tried to adjust her aim. But it was too late. A coffee mug slammed right into Nicole's hand. Maybe it was the impact or the surprise of the attack, but Nicole dropped the gun.

Pete went after it.

So did Beck.

Both of them scrambled across the floor toward it.

Above them, Nicole moved as well. Faith, too. Beck could hear Faith's footsteps, and he knew she was going after Nicole.

And Faith might get hurt in the process.

Beck caught onto Pete and slammed him against the floor. Nicole reached down, to help Pete or get the gun. But reaching was as far as she got. Faith grabbed Nicole and with a fierce jerk, she yanked her back. It was the break that Beck needed. His hand clamped around the gun, and this time, he came up ready to fire.

"Move back," Beck told Faith.

Nicole reached for her to try to use her as a shield, but Faith darted across the room just out of Nicole's reach.

"Don't move," Beck warned Pete when he tried to get up. His brother turned his head, and their gazes connected.

Beck made sure there were no doubts or hesitation in his eyes. Because there certainly wasn't any of that in his heart.

"I will kill you," Beck promised.

Pete laid his head on the floor and put his hands on the back of his head. Finally surrendering.

# Chapter Sixteen

Faith frantically checked Aubrey again.

She hadn't seen any blood, or even a scratch, but she had to be sure that Pete's shots hadn't harmed her child.

"No, no, no," Aubrey fussed, batting Faith's hands away. The little girl rubbed her eyes and yawned. She was obviously sleepy and didn't want any more of this impromptu exam.

Deputy Winston rushed in the door. He had his weapon drawn, and he hurried past them and into the kitchen. A moment later, the Ranger, Sgt. McKinney, followed. Then Deputy Gafford.

Finally!

Even though it'd been only minutes since her nine-one-one call, Beck now had the backup he needed. And once she had the all clear that it was safe to check on him, she would. Well, she would after Marita had taken Aubrey into the bedroom away from Nicole and Pete.

She prayed Beck was all right.

In the distance she heard the sirens from an ambulance. And she heard footsteps. Faith looked up from her now fussy daughter and spotted Beck.

Oh, God. He was bleeding. There was a gash on his forehead. His left cheek. And both hands were bloodied.

"The ambulance will be here any minute," Faith told him.

He looked at her. Then at Aubrey. He seemed to make it to them in one giant step, and he pulled them both into his arms. Faith's breath shattered, and she was afraid she wouldn't be able to hold back the tears of relief.

"Is she hurt?" Beck asked. His voice was frantic. "Are you hurt?"

Faith pulled back so she could meet his gaze. "We're not hurt. You are. I called the ambulance for you."

His breath swooshed out. "You're not hurt." He repeated it several times and drew them back into his embrace.

Aubrey rubbed her eyes again and babbled something. It sounded cranky, and Faith figured she was about to cry, but her daughter maneuvered her way into Beck's arms and dropped her head on his shoulder.

"I'll see if I can be of assistance in the kitchen," Tracy volunteered, trying to give them some privacy.

"Want me to take Aubrey?" Marita asked.

"No," Faith and Beck said in unison.

"All right then. I'll just go outside and let the EMTs know what's going on." Marita took a step and then stopped. Her forehead was bunched up. "What exactly is going on?"

He and Faith exchanged glances. He didn't let go of her. But then she had no plans to let go of him either.

"My brother is about to be arrested for three murders," Beck explained. "Nicole will be taken into custody as well since she tried to assist him with his escape.

And we need to look for Darin. He's out there somewhere and needs medical attention."

"Oh. I see." Marita turned pale. She waggled her fingers toward the sound of the sirens. "What should I tell the EMT guys? They'll be here any minute."

"Have then come in and check out Faith," Beck insisted.

Other than some bruises and maybe a scrape or two, Faith knew she was fine. She couldn't say the same for Beck. He'd need stitches for that gash.

"And I want them to check out Beck," Faith added as Marita went out the door.

"I'm okay," he insisted, kissing Aubrey's cheek. He kissed Faith's, too. "At least now I am. For a minute there, I thought I'd lost you."

"Me, too," she managed to say. Her emotion was too raw to talk about.

There was movement from the kitchen, and a moment later, Pete appeared. Handcuffed. Corey had a hold on him. The other deputy had Nicole cuffed and was walking her to the front door.

Pete stopped, and Beck automatically turned so that Aubrey wouldn't be near the man. "There's nothing we have to say to each other," Beck insisted.

But Pete didn't speak right away. He stood there, volleying glances among Beck, Aubrey and Faith. "You fell hard for her, didn't you?" He didn't wait for Beck to confirm it. "That's how I feel about Nicole."

"You were ready to kill her," Faith pointed out.

"I wouldn't have. *Couldn't* have," he corrected. "Love really messes you up." His attention landed on Aubrey again. "I know she's Sherry's kid. Sherry showed me her picture. One she'd taken in a park, and she tried to convince me that I was the one who got her pregnant."

That gave Faith another jolt of adrenaline. "Did you?"

Pete shook his head. "Not a chance."

Faith desperately wanted to believe him. "And since you've been so truthful in the past, I should just take you at your word?"

"He's telling the truth," Corey volunteered. "This time, anyway. I saw the DNA results from the Ranger lab. He's not the father. Neither are you, Beck. It's Nolan Wheeler."

*Nolan.* In hindsight, it didn't surprise her. Not really. Sherry had spent most of her life breaking up and then getting back together with Nolan.

"He might have fathered her," Beck mumbled. "But Nolan was never her father."

Faith couldn't have agreed more. If the man hadn't been dead, his DNA connection to Aubrey would have caused her stomach to go into a tailspin. Because Nolan would have spent the rest of his life trying to figure out ways to use Aubrey to get what he wanted.

"Get my brother out of here," Beck instructed the deputy.

Pete didn't protest. He looked straight ahead as he was escorted out. Nicole was next. She didn't even try to say anything. Tears were streaming down her cheeks, and she made a series of hoarse sobs.

However, Deputy Gafford did stop. "On the way over, I got a call from the hospital. Darin Matthews is back there. He's not hurt, and he wanted me to check on Faith, to make sure she was all right."

Faith was so glad that Beck was holding on to her.

Her brother was safe. Pete hadn't hurt him. And better yet, he was receiving the medical treatment he needed. She would check on him as soon as things had settled down.

Whenever that might be.

It might take her years to forget how close she'd come to losing Beck and Aubrey.

"The other Texas Ranger is with Darin now," the deputy continued. "Will there be any charges filed against him?"

"No," Beck quickly answered. "But I want him to have a thorough psychiatric evaluation."

The deputy nodded and escorted Nicole out.

Faith looked around and realized they were alone. The house was quiet. Her heart rate was slowly returning to normal.

"Are you really okay?" Beck asked.

But the silence didn't last. Before she could answer, there was the sound of hurried footsteps, and she automatically braced herself for the worst.

Roy came rushing through the front door.

He looked at Beck. At Aubrey. Then at her. He'd no doubt passed his other son and daughter-in-law and knew they were under arrest. But his concern seemed to be aimed at Beck.

"Son, you're bleeding," Roy greeted him.

"Just a scratch," Beck assured him.

"He needs stitches," Faith insisted.

Roy agreed with a nod, and he put his hands on his hips. He looked around, as if he didn't know what to say or do. "I just spoke to Corey and the nanny, Marita. They told me what happened in here."

"Yeah," was all Beck said.

"'i," Aubrey babbled to Roy.

There were tears in Roy's eyes, but he forced a smile when he returned the "hi." He hesitated. "I'm sorry. So sorry for what Pete did. I knew about the blackmail and the payoff, but I swear I didn't know he'd killed those people. And I didn't know he would come after the three of you. I'm sorry," he repeated, aiming this one at Faith.

She gave his arm a gentle squeeze. "Thank you."

Roy turned those tearful eyes to Beck. "What can I do? Give me something to do. I can't go home and sit there."

"You can go to my office and call Pete and Nicole a lawyer. They're going to need one."

"Of course. I'll do that. And if you need anything, just let me know."

"I will."

"Make sure he sees the medics," Roy whispered to Faith. He gave her arm a gentle squeeze as well and went back out the door just as the medics were coming in.

Beck held up his hand to stop them. "Could you give me a few minutes?" he asked.

That halted the two men in their tracks, and they looked at her for verification. "Just a few minutes," she bargained. But only a few. She wanted that gash checked.

Aubrey fussed and babbled, "Bye-bye," but Faith didn't think she wanted to go with Roy or the medics. She smeared her fist over her eyes again and whimpered.

"It's okay," Beck said to Aubrey, and he lightly circled his fingers over her back.

"Da, Da, Da, Da," Aubrey answered. Not in a happy

tone, either. But it was a tone Faith recognized. Her baby was on the verge of a tired tantrum.

Beck must have sensed that because he caught onto Faith's arm and led them to the sofa. Once he'd sat down, he moved Aubrey so that her tummy was against his chest. She dropped her head onto his shoulder and stuck her thumb in her mouth. Within seconds, her eyelids were already lowering.

Faith smiled. "Tantrum averted," she whispered. Good. She didn't have any energy left to deal with anything. "I might have to call you the next time she gets fussy."

Beck angled his eyes in her direction and stared at her. She'd thought the light comment would have given him some relief. It was certainly better than the alternative of her falling apart.

"You said you loved me," Beck reminded her.

That kicked up her heart again. She'd planned on having this discussion later. After some of the chaos had settled. "Yes, I did say that." Because she wanted to dodge eye contact with him, she checked Aubrey. Sound asleep.

"You meant it?"

But before he let her answer, he leaned in and kissed her. He winced because his lip was busted. Hers, too, she realized when his mouth touched hers. She didn't care. That kiss was worth a little pain, and it was the ultimate truth serum. She was going to lay her heart out there and let him know exactly how she felt about him.

She hoped he wouldn't laugh.

Or run the other direction.

"I meant it," she answered. "I love you." Beck and Aubrey were two things in her life that she was certain of. "I'm crazy in love with you."

His face relaxed a bit. The corner of his mouth even lifted in a near smile. "Good. Because I'm crazy in love with you, too."

A sharp sound of surprise leaped from her mouth. "Really?" She heard her voice. Heard the shock. "You're sure it's not just the lust talking?"

"The lust is there," he admitted. He reached out and pushed her hair away from her face. "But so is the love. You did me the honor of letting me be your first lover. Now I'm asking if you'll let me be your last."

*Mercy.* That was not a light tone. Nor a light look in his eyes. Still, Faith approached that comment with caution. "Are you asking me to go steady?" she joked.

"No. I'm asking you to marry me."

Oh. *Wow.*

Her heart went crazy. So did her stomach. Her breathing. Her entire body.

Was this really happening? She wanted it to happen. Desperately wanted it, she realized. But she hadn't expected it.

As if to convince her, he kissed her again. And again. Until he was the only thing she could think of. Beck had that kind of effect on her. He could make even the aftermath of chaos seem incredible. Heat and love just rippled through her.

"I don't want you to call me when Aubrey's fussy because I want to be there, close by, to hear her myself. I want to be her father, and I want to be your husband."

"You're already her father," Faith said. And it was true. "Aubrey chose you herself." She had to blink back happy tears. "She made a good choice."

"I'm glad you think so. Now, to the rest. I want to

be your last lover. Your only lover. What do you think about that?"

Faith didn't have to think. She knew. There was only one answer. "Yes."

\* \* \* \* \*

**TEXAS PATERNITY: BOOTS AND BOOTIES**
*continues next month with*
*EXPECTING TROUBLE, only from Delores Fossen*
*and Harlequin Intrigue.*

Celebrate 60 years of pure reading pleasure with
Harlequin® Books!

Harlequin Romance® is celebrating by showering
you with DIAMOND BRIDES in February 2009.
Six stories that promise to bring a touch of sparkle to
your life, with diamond proposals and dazzling
weddings, sparkling brides and gorgeous grooms!

Enjoy a sneak peek at Caroline Anderson's
TWO LITTLE MIRACLES,
available February 2009
from Harlequin Romance®.

"I'VE FOUND HER."

Max froze.

It was what he'd been waiting for since June, but now—now he was almost afraid to voice the question. His heart stalling, he leaned slowly back in his chair and scoured the investigator's face for clues. "Where?" he asked, and his voice sounded rough and unused, like a rusty hinge.

"In Suffolk. She's living in a cottage."

*Living.* His heart crashed back to life, and he sucked in a long, slow breath. All these months he'd feared—

"Is she well?"

"Yes, she's well."

He had to force himself to ask the next question. "Alone?"

The man paused. "No. The cottage belongs to a man called John Blake. He's working away at the moment, but he comes and goes."

God. He felt sick. So sick he hardly registered the next few words, but then gradually they sank in. "She's got *what?*"

"Babies. Twin girls. They're eight months old."

"Eight—?" he echoed under his breath. "They must be his."

He was thinking out loud, but the P.I. heard and corrected him.

"Apparently not. I gather they're hers. She's been there since mid-January last year, and they were born during the summer—June, the woman in the post office thought. She was more than helpful. I think there's been a certain amount of speculation about their relationship."

He'd just bet there had. God, he was going to kill her. Or Blake. Maybe both of them.

"Of course, looking at the dates, she was presumably pregnant when she left you, so they could be yours, or she could have been having an affair with this Blake character before…"

He glared at the unfortunate P.I. "Just stick to your job. I can do the math," he snapped, swallowing the unpalatable possibility that she'd been unfaithful to him before she'd left. "Where is she? I want the address."

"It's all in here," the man said, sliding a large envelope across the desk to him. "With my invoice."

"I'll get it seen to. Thank you."

"If there's anything else you need, Mr. Gallagher, any further information—"

"I'll be in touch."

"The woman in the post office told me Blake was away at the moment, if that helps," he added quietly, and opened the door.

Max stared down at the envelope, hardly daring to open it, but when the door clicked softly shut behind the

P.I., he eased up the flap, tipped it and felt his breath jam in his throat as the photos spilled out over the desk.

Oh, Lord, she looked gorgeous. Different, though. It took him a moment to recognize her, because she'd grown her hair, and it was tied back in a ponytail, making her look younger and somehow freer. The blond highlights were gone, and it was back to its natural soft golden-brown, with a little curl in the end of the ponytail that he wanted to thread his finger through and tug, just gently, to draw her back to him.

Crazy. She'd put on a little weight, but it suited her. She looked well and happy and beautiful, but oddly, considering how desperate he'd been for news of her for the past year—one year, three weeks and two days, to be exact—it wasn't only Julia who held his attention after the initial shock. It was the babies sitting side by side in a supermarket trolley. Two identical and absolutely beautiful little girls.

\* \* \* \* \*

When Max Gallagher hires a P.I. to find his estranged wife, Julia, he discovers she's not alone— she has twin baby girls, and they might be his. Now workaholic Max has just two weeks to prove that he can be a wonderful husband and father to the family he wants to treasure.

*Look for TWO LITTLE MIRACLES*
*by Caroline Anderson,*
*available February 2009 from Harlequin Romance®.*

# CELEBRATE
## 60 YEARS
### OF PURE READING PLEASURE
## WITH **HARLEQUIN®**!

**We'll be spotlighting a different series
every month throughout 2009
to celebrate our 60th anniversary.**

**Look for Harlequin® Romance in February!**

**Harlequin® Romance is celebrating by showering
you with Diamond Brides in February 2009.**

Six stories that promise to bring a touch of sparkle to
your life, with diamond proposals and dazzling weddings,
sparkling brides and gorgeous grooms!

Collect all six books in February 2009,
featuring *Two Little Miracles* by Caroline Anderson.

*Look for the Diamond Brides miniseries
in February 2009!*

# HARLEQUIN® Romance®

This February the Harlequin® Romance series will feature six Diamond Brides stories featuring diamond proposals and gorgeous grooms.

## *Share your dream wedding proposal and you could WIN!*

The most romantic entry will win a diamond necklace and will inspire a proposal in one of our upcoming Diamond Grooms books in 2010.

In 100 words or less, tell us the most romantic way that you dream of being proposed to.

For more information, and to enter the Diamond Brides Proposal contest, please visit
**www.DiamondBridesProposal.com**

Or mail your entry to us at:

IN THE U.S.: 3010 Walden Ave., P.O. Box 9069, Buffalo, NY 14269-9069
IN CANADA: 225 Duncan Mill Road, Don Mills, ON M3B 3K9

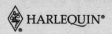

# REQUEST YOUR FREE BOOKS!

## 2 FREE NOVELS PLUS 2 FREE GIFTS!

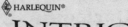

HARLEQUIN®

## INTRIGUE®

### Breathtaking Romantic Suspense

**YES!** Please send me 2 FREE Harlequin Intrigue® novels and my 2 FREE gifts (gifts are worth about $10). After receiving them, if I don't wish to receive any more books, I can return the shipping statement marked "cancel." If I don't cancel, I will receive 6 brand-new novels every month and be billed just $4.24 per book in the U.S. or $4.99 per book in Canada, plus 25¢ shipping and handling per book and applicable taxes, if any*. That's a savings of close to 15% off the cover price! I understand that accepting the 2 free books and gifts places me under no obligation to buy anything. I can always return a shipment and cancel at any time. Even if I never buy another book from Harlequin, the two free books and gifts are mine to keep forever.

182 HDN EEZ7  382 HDN EEZK

| | | |
|---|---|---|
| Name | (PLEASE PRINT) | |
| Address | | Apt. # |
| City | State/Prov. | Zip/Postal Code |

Signature (if under 18, a parent or guardian must sign)

Mail to the **Harlequin Reader Service:**
**IN U.S.A.:** P.O. Box 1867, Buffalo, NY  14240-1867
**IN CANADA:** P.O. Box 609, Fort Erie, Ontario  L2A 5X3

Not valid to current subscribers of Harlequin Intrigue books.

**Want to try two free books from another line?**
**Call 1-800-873-8635 or visit www.morefreebooks.com.**

\* Terms and prices subject to change without notice. N.Y. residents add applicable sales tax. Canadian residents will be charged applicable provincial taxes and GST. Offer not valid in Quebec. This offer is limited to one order per household. All orders subject to approval. Credit or debit balances in a customer's account(s) may be offset by any other outstanding balance owed by or to the customer. Please allow 4 to 6 weeks for delivery. Offer available while quantities last.

**Your Privacy:** Harlequin is committed to protecting your privacy. Our Privacy Policy is available online at www.eHarlequin.com or upon request from the Reader Service. From time to time we make our lists of customers available to reputable third parties who may have a product or service of interest to you. If you would prefer we not share your name and address, please check here. ☐

HI08R

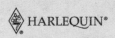